CW00864327

THE BOOKS
— OF —
NORENE III
Final Fight

Jane Sefc

authorHOUSE

AuthorHouse™ UK
1663 Liberty Drive
Bloomington, IN 47403 USA
www.authorhouse.co.uk
Phone: 0800 047 8203 (Domestic TFN)
*   +44 1908 723714 (International)*

Published by AuthorHouse 11/18/2019

ISBN: 978-1-7283-9575-3 (sc)
ISBN: 978-1-7283-9574-6 (hc)
ISBN: 978-1-7283-9578-4 (e)

To Vlady,
for his love and his support.

THE STORY UP TO NOW

In the previous two parts of this trilogy, a stranger with green glowing eyes, going under the name Rex, wanted to get a magical necklace. The necklace had had been possessed by three owners. The first was the owner of the fortress Strongfort from whom Amy, Rex's sidekick, stole it. She lost it when she ran from the fortress. The necklace fell into a river and travelled all the way from Wolfast to Norene where a curious wolf found it. The necklace and an attack by a werewolf changed the wolf into human. He chose the name Daniel and tried to blend in with humans.

Rex persuaded Mors, the leader of Wolfast, to attack Norene. The young king of Norene, Ethan, had to fight for his country only a few days after his coronation. He lost the first fight, but his remaining lords took him to safety.

Daniel became friends with Charles, and their path crossed Ethan's. They joined Ethan in his quest to win Norene back and succeeded. Ethan took a liking to both Daniel and Charles. He made Charles a lord and invited Daniel to live anywhere he wanted.

Daniel gave the necklace to Ethan. However, Rex wasn't the only one who wanted it. A Masked Man came to Royal City like a hurricane, causing a lot of trouble.

Edmund, who was responsible for the content of *The Royal Messenger*, hired his friend's son, John, as an illustrator. He asked another employee, Christine, to keep an eye on him, but Christine was more curious about the Masked Man. John was getting on her nerves, but when the Masked Man attacked the king and then later her, she accepted help even from clumsy and idiotic John.

Trying to find out about the Masked Man proved to be dangerous as more dead bodies appeared. But it was never clear where the Masked Man's loyalties were. All he wanted was the necklace, but the necklace was lost again. No one knew where it was.

CHAPTER 1

Amy walked to a tall building and stopped next to the front door. It was the middle of the night, and the jeweller's shop was closed. She looked around, but there was no one else on the street. She was dressed in her usual tight black shirt and trousers. Her dark hair was gathered up beneath a cap, and her face was covered by a black mask. If she wanted to, she could blend in with the darkness around her.

She looked up. There was an open window above the store. She wasn't sure if the shop owner had forgotten the window was open or hadn't expected anyone would be able to climb that high. But it didn't matter. It was her ticket in. Quietly, she jumped on to the façade of the house and used the ornaments to climb the building. Amy reached the window as easily as some people walk up the stairs. She heaved herself onto the ledge and looked inside. When she recognized that she was in a kitchen, she slid off the ledge and sneaked through to the hall. She walked close to the wall because the wooden floor could creak beneath her feet, and she didn't want to wake anyone up. As she reached the front door, she heard the floor creaking in another room.

In a panic, she looked around. The hall was completely empty, void of any furniture. The closest door was the one from which the sound of steps was coming. She didn't want to jump outside. The owner would immediately notice if the front door suddenly closed or was left open. There was no way she could get through the door without attracting the owner's attention. She therefore placed her hands on the wall in front of her and quickly jumped onto the opposite wall. She climbed the wall as if it weren't vertical at all. The moment she was at the same level as the top of the entrance door, the door to her right opened. An elderly man in a nightgown stepped out and walked over to the kitchen, dragging his feet.

Amy quickly used the time to climb all the way to the ceiling. She could hear pouring water, and then the man almost immediately emerged into the hall, yawning. He held a glass of water in his hand as he shuffled back to the bedroom.

Amy waited a little while after the man had closed the door of the bedroom. When she was sure that he wasn't coming back anytime soon, she jumped down, landing noiselessly on the floor. Slowly and carefully, she turned the key in the lock and opened the door. She was afraid that it might creak, but the door opened noiselessly. She looked into the dark hallway ahead of her and stepped out of the flat. Carefully, she closed the door behind her.

The hallway was pitch black with only a tiny window up high. The light from the streetlights couldn't reach all the way there, and only a small ray of moonshine penetrated the darkness. Amy had trouble distinguishing her surroundings. She felt her way to a staircase she assumed led to the store.

She hurried as fast down the stairs as the darkness allowed her. Finally, she reached the bottom and found a closed door. She tried the handle, but the door was locked. She cursed under her breath. She had never been good at picking locks, and she wouldn't even try it in a dark corridor such as this. Quietly, she felt her way back to the flat and carefully opened the front door. She froze, listening to the silence of the night. The flat was quiet. A quick search of the walls revealed a big key on a small hook next to the door. Amy took it and once again left the flat, closing the door behind her. This time she found the staircase faster and didn't even need to feel her way through the darkness.

She reached the bottom of the stairs and, using her hands, found the lock. She tried not to make a single sound as she slid the key into the lock. She turned the key, and a quiet click followed. The door creaked as she opened it. She looked nervously up at the door of the flat and then rushed into the store, closing the door behind her. Another creak was followed by a thud. The sounds seemed so loud to her. She locked the door and pressed her ear against it, listening to the hallway behind it. No sound came.

She heaved a sigh of relief and turned around. The streetlight, along with some moonlight, shone into the store through three tall windows. In the dim light she could see that the place was very tidy. There were some glass-fronted shelves near the windows on the other side of the room, and a counter made out of low cabinets with glass on top stood in the middle.

Amy tiptoed to the display and quickly scanned its contents. She couldn't make out too much detail in the dim light, but she saw enough. There were mainly rings displayed. She didn't waste too much time there. Even if someone had already brought the necklace, the jeweller wouldn't have displayed it. Amy assumed that a person who would find the necklace and actually sell it wouldn't be from the upper class. The jeweller wouldn't mind buying the necklace from the person, probably paying much less than what he thought it was worth, but he would know to keep it out of sight for a while. It could still be stolen.

If someone had already sold the necklace to the jeweller, it would be locked up somewhere. There had to be a safe in the room. She turned to the walls, looking for anything that might be a hidden safe. There was a painting of a house in a forest on the wall. Amy was doubtful. It was very unlikely that the solitary and way-too-obvious painting hid any secrets. But she lifted the corner of the frame and peeped behind the canvas. She was right. There was only the wall behind it. She let go of the painting and looked around. The lock on the front door rattled. She spun around and jumped behind the counter. She could still see the room from this spot and keep hidden, but if the person lit a torch or moved around the place in a quick pace, she was trapped.

She watched the door, her heart beating painfully in her chest. She couldn't make out who was standing behind the glass door, but she had a feeling that the person wore a hat. She dreaded the possibility that it might be the Masked Man.

The door opened, and Amy nearly gasped. She clapped her hand over her mouth to keep from making any sound, and she watched as the Masked Man entered the room. He closed the door behind him and looked around. He didn't bother to crouch. His face was covered with a piece of cloth, and his eyes were in a constant shadow cast by his hat.

Amy continued to crouch as she waited for the Masked Man to take the first step. He stood still for a while, looking around. His gaze stopped on the display behind which Amy was hidden. With a swift movement, he stepped behind the counter. Amy had barely enough time to move to the other side of the counter and out of sight. The Masked Man stopped behind the counter. Just as Amy had, he looked at the display. He stood still, not seeing anything else in the room. Amy tried to keep as still as possible. Any movement in the Masked Man's field of view would attract his attention immediately. It felt like ages, but he finally turned around and looked at the wall behind him. He lifted the painting and let it fall back down. Amy suspected that, if she could see his face, there would be disappointment on it.

The Masked Man moved to the other side of the store, and Amy crawled back behind the counter. The Masked Man turned around and looked at the counter. Amy crouched lower and waited. When he didn't approach her, she risked another glance. He was crouching above a chest in the corner by the front door, studying the chest's contents. He closed the chest, making sure that the lid didn't produce any sound, and then he walked outside, not wasting another glance at the room. He peered in to the street, and when he made sure it was empty, he closed the door and locked it.

Amy heaved a sigh of relief and sat on the floor, leaning against the counter. Her heart was beating hard, and only now did she dare to breathe deeply again. She waited for her heart rate to return to normal and then sneaked outside through the owner's flat, leaving everything the way she had found it.

As she stepped onto the empty street, she frowned. She was supposed to check the two jewellers in the city, but she was curious about what the Masked Man was up to. So she decided to tail him. It seemed he had a plan. He was good at being like a shadow, though not as good as Amy. If she could find him, she might be able to tail him. And then she would know what he knew.

Christine wanted to hurry to John, but she didn't dare leave the warehouse till dawn. She had no idea where Rex was, and the possibility of bumping into him was scary. She wanted to wait for daytime. Rex would probably be hidden somewhere, and there would be people on the streets. So she sat behind the crates, stretching her legs from time to time, and watched the high windows for signs of dawn.

She didn't feel sleepy at all. Many thoughts ran through her mind, and she had trouble sorting them out. She needed to tell someone what was going on, preferably John. She needed to get it out of her head. She thought of walking up and down the warehouse; walking often helped her think. But she didn't dare step out from her hiding place. True, it wasn't the best possible hiding place in the world, since the crates were the only ones in the warehouse, but at least she wouldn't be spotted right away. She looked at the windows which still didn't show the slightest signs of morning. She wished she had a clock. She wondered if it would be safe to leave the warehouse and go home.

Suddenly, she jumped with start and looked around in surprise. She was still in the warehouse, but there was finally daylight inside. She must have dozed off and slept the rest of the night. She hurried outside, happy that the night was over. People were already in the streets, merchants had opened their stores and stalls, and the Royal Guards were patrolling on every street. She actually liked the busyness of the city, this morning in particular. The sun was already quite high when she finally barged into John's building. She hurried up the stairs and didn't even wait to catch her breath. Out of the corner of her eye, she saw the door to Miss Luisa's flat open. She didn't stop to greet her. She stopped only in front of John's door on the second floor, banged on the door, and leaned against the door frame, fighting for her breath.

John opened the door, and his jaw dropped when he saw a dirty and dishevelled Christine in front of him. She hadn't seen her reflection on her way to John's, but she suspected that she looked awful. That could be expected after spending a whole night on the floor of the warehouse. John was already dressed for work, looking rather dashing. The air of a boy from a farm was nowhere to be seen.

"What happened?" he asked, surprised, as he stepped back. Christine staggered inside and sat gratefully on the bed. John hurried to the corner and poured a glass of water from a jug. He handed it to her.

"I witnessed a conversation between the Masked Man and some woman," Christine said, and she drank water lustily. When the glass was empty, she stopped and took a deep breath. John looked a little pale, and his farm origin was once again noticeable in his posture. She wondered whether she was starting to like him and that was the reason she sometimes didn't notice the "farmness" about him. Maybe the city was having a little influence on him.

"What did they talk about?" John asked breathlessly.

"I don't remember word for word, but it seems that the Masked Man is a good guy."

John relaxed a little and leaned against the table. "I thought that he attacked the king and killed several men," he said calmly. "How can he be a good guy?"

"He didn't attack the king. Or at least I don't think he did. That's how I understood the conversation. Maybe I'm wrong. And you yourself pointed out that the only thing that the Masked Man and the king's attacker had in common was the hat, the coat, and the cloth over his face. These are not disguises that would be difficult to find in the city. It crossed my mind that, since the Masked Man was already in the city, the attacker could have chosen a similar outfit to look like him. On purpose, you know. But that's now beside the point. I found out that a guy named Rex is behind all this. I even saw him after the Masked Man left."

"He was there?" John asked, and he bolted upright.

Christine looked up in surprise. "You know him?"

"You don't?" John asked even more surprised. Christine shot him a black look. John sighed and sat down next to her, turning to face her. "He's the guy who was behind that short war with Wolfast. It seems that he's still after something. I wouldn't be surprised if he's behind the attack on the king."

"How do you know this?" Christine asked stunned.

"Edmund told me on my first day. Captain Stuart mentioned the guy to him when he was searching the place for *The Freedom Speaker*."

"Why didn't Edmund tell me?" Christine asked, clutching the glass in her hands. She held it in front of her as a shield.

John looked down at the glass. "Maybe he thought that you knew already," he said with a shrug. He looked away. "You will have to ask Edmund, but since you know so much, he might be surprised that you didn't know this."

"I didn't know until you told me," Christine snapped. She put the glass on the floor by the bed. "Be that as it may, I didn't like Rex one bit. There's something strange about him, something sinister. Something I thought that I would see in the Masked Man."

"What did he say?"

Christine had to think hard about the previous night. "The Masked Man said that he was keeping an eye on things," she said. John opened his mouth to say something, but then changed his mind and closed it again. "He told them to leave the king out of it," Christine continued. "The woman seemed to be scared of him. She's the one who hired the men, and the Masked Man was tracking them down and disposing of them."

"And what did Rex say?"

"He had been hidden there and showed up a little later. He had heard the whole conversation. He seemed angry. His eyes actually glow! I've never seen anything like it. He said that the Masked Man had to have been warned; otherwise, he wouldn't have been there fast enough. He kept on talking about someone called Fortis, but I don't think that's the Masked Man. And he told the woman to watch the city jewellers. Rex believes that anyone who found the necklace will try to sell it. I only wish I knew how to get in touch with the Masked Man."

"What good would that do?" John asked, surprised. "He still killed all those men, even if he didn't attack the king. He's most likely very dangerous. Furthermore, you have no idea where he lives or hides. We can't go and search the whole city!"

"No, we can't," Christine said with a slow nod. "But we can go and inform Captain Stuart about everything. Maybe his men can."

"Oh, I don't know," John said doubtfully. "I heard that the captain is a piece of work. What if he's with Rex on this? And even if we went to him, why should he believe us?"

"I don't know, but it's a start. The other option is to go to the city and look for the Masked Man ourselves."

"I don't think either of those is a good idea," John said pensively. "The first option—and let's say for the sake of argument that the captain is really on the king's side—might have the opposite effect. The Royal Guards think that the Masked Man attacked the king. They are after him because they believe he's a criminal. And let's face it, with so many dead people and the trouble he's caused, he might as well be. However, right now it seems that he's the only thing that can stop Rex. If he's locked up, that could cause a lot of trouble. And explaining the situation to the captain won't ensure that he understands all of this. I didn't get the idea that he particularly liked us, so I see no reason why he should listen to us." He took a deep breath. "The second option is even crazier. First, as we both agreed, it's impossible to search the whole city, and second, what if Rex or that woman see you? You don't want to become too easy target. You shouldn't wander about the city until this is resolved."

"You're right, of course, but I can't just sit at home and do nothing! What if the Masked Man fails? What if Rex gets too close to the king? I bet the king would believe us." Christine suddenly froze and looked at the wall with a faraway look. "That's an idea," she said slowly. "I will tell the king everything. I know that the king would believe our story, no matter how crazy it sounds. He's not so sceptical."

"You want to get an audience with the king?" John asked flatly, and his jaw fell.

"Yes! That's the option for me. I wouldn't be risking anything, and I can explain the situation without prejudice on the king's part."

"The king was attacked by a Masked Man," John pointed out. He leaned closer so that his face was only inches away from Christine's. She didn't move away. "What makes you think he won't hold a grudge? He might think that it's still the same man, and he might want to catch him. On top of that, why do you think that the king wouldn't judge us as crazy? I met him only once in that corridor. He seemed nice, but I wouldn't bet anything that he would believe us."

"I know this may sound crazy," Christine said, leaning closer, "but he's the king. He's the one looking after his people. He's our hero of the last month. He *will* listen. It's … it just is like that with kings."

"I think that you're idealizing him," John whispered. They were nearly touching with their noses.

"Maybe," Christine said hesitantly, and she pulled back a little. "I will start with the information that it's not the same man," she said more confidently. "And based on the king's reaction, I can then tell him everything or leave. What do you think?"

"I don't see why it's the only option," John said doubtfully.

"We know that the king is not with Rex," Christine explained. "And I just know that he's open to information. He's smart. He can use that information with everything he knows, and being a king, he is well informed. Trust me on this one! If we manage to persuade him, he can order the captain to search for Rex but not arrest him."

"He can also order the captain to kill the guy."

"He won't. Call it a hunch, but I know he won't."

John thought for a while, watching Christine intently. She held her breath, awaiting his verdict. Then he smiled at her. "I think you're incredible," he said. "I just love your enthusiasm and optimism. People like you make a difference in the world—by action and by passion."

Christine smiled at him brightly, pleased with his praise. Her heart started to beat faster, and her face warmed up. She felt good about herself. No, she felt great! It was a good plan, and she knew it would work. It was definitely better than sitting at home, waiting. And John thought so too. She noticed that John's eyes were a very nice shade of blue. His smile was cute, too. She liked him at the moment. He wasn't a small-village boy now.

They stared into each other's eyes for a long time. Christine thought of looking away, but she liked those eyes. There was a spark in them. She felt safe in John's presence—safe and calm. The world was no longer scary, and the Masked Man and Rex, with all the trouble they had brought, were far away. She only now realized that she considered John a friend, even though it had been only a few days. True, there had been moments when he had been weird and had gotten on her nerves. And there had been moments when he had caused a lot of trouble and she'd wanted to kill him. But when he was calm like this, she wanted to hug him.

John watched Christine with a smile on his face that made Christine's knees weak. She glanced at his lips and back into his blue eyes. She wondered what it would be like to kiss him. An excitement ran through her body at the mere thought. Suddenly, John's smile froze. For a moment he looked as if he wanted to say something. Then he jumped to his feet and turned his back to Christine. "We can walk to work together," he said, walking towards the table in the corner. Christine watched his back, not sure what to think. The moment was gone, and the warmth and calmness had been pushed aside by a wave of a whole range of emotions.

"I think I'll go home and get cleaned up and sleep a little," Christine said, trying to sound nonchalant. "I was up all night, after all. Please, tell Edmund that I will come in tomorrow." She wondered what had happened.

She had a feeling that John liked her, but now she wasn't sure of her own feelings. Maybe it was all just a result of feeling lost with the Masked Man and finding a solution to her problem. That had to be it.

John still hadn't turned towards her. He fiddled with something in the drawer of the table beneath the window, his back resolutely turned to her. "Let me escort you, then," he said in an even voice. Christine frowned. He hadn't sounded nervous or confused; he had sounded angry. She tried to remember what they had been talking about. There was no reason for John to be angry. She hadn't tried to do anything; they had just had a brief "moment". Christine sighed, shaking her head. Anger was filling her. She stood up and shot John a black look. If he wanted to act all hurt and pretend that she'd done something wrong, he could do that alone.

"That won't be necessary," she snapped at him, and she marched to the door. She grabbed the handle and looked over her shoulder at John. He was frozen by the table with his back to her, his head slightly turned so that he could see her in his peripheral vision. She froze with her hand on the handle. They both stood still for a few seconds. Christine hoped that John would stop her from leaving or at least would turn to look at her, but he didn't do anything.

Christine cursed under her breath and opened the door. She stepped outside and slammed the door behind her with all her strength. The anger was bubbling inside her. Why should she care what that farm boy thought? She fumed as she ran down the stairs, trying to convince herself that she didn't care.

As she reached the middle of the stairs, the door to her left opened, and Miss Luisa stepped into the corridor. She was glaring at Christine who was stumping down the stairs. Normally, Christine wouldn't have cared, but Miss Luisa wasn't someone you chose to ignore. Her mere presence made you a nice, law-abiding person. Her scowl made you scared for your life.

Christine forced herself to smile as she wished Miss Luisa good morning before she hurried out of the building. As the front door closed after Christine, the smile vanished from her lips. She looked up at the window of John's flat, expecting to see him there. He wasn't.

If he wanted to act like a little boy, it was his choice. He had to learn what life was about. And she wasn't going to teach him anything. He had to grow up on his own!

CHAPTER 2

Bess's coach arrived in a little town and stopped in front of an inn. Bess wasn't hungry, but it was a good opportunity to find out what news was circling in the area. Besides, even though Bess wasn't hungry, it didn't mean that his coachman, Finn, wasn't. He was a young skinny boy with red hair and a lot of freckles on his nose. He looked like he needed to eat a lot.

Bess stepped out of the coach and looked around. A few curious faces appeared in the windows on the other side of the road. Finn fixed the reins to the coach and jumped down. He turned to open door for Bess, but when he saw that Bess was already out of the coach, he turned around and walked over to the horses.

Bess turned towards the inn and looked up at the plaque over the door. The inn was called Werewolf's Lair. Bess's eyes narrowed. If he had noticed the sign before, he wouldn't have asked Finn to stop there. Now that they had stopped, it seemed ridiculous to continue their drive without a proper meal. He sighed and entered the inn. The innkeeper stood by a table nearby, wiping it clean. There were only two customers inside, each sitting at a different table and silently eating a meal. Everyone looked up and froze when the door closed behind Bess with a slap. The innkeeper turned pale at the sight of Bess. He watched him with his jaw hanging open as he slowly continued to wipe the table.

"Good evening," Bess said with a smile. The two men at the tables returned to their meals, looking very nervous. "Could we get something to eat?" he asked with a smile, and he motioned to the coach where Finn was checking the wheels. The innkeeper looked at the coach and then back at Bess. "Is it also possible to get some hay for the horses? And some water?" Bess asked. The innkeeper didn't say anything; neither did he nod. He only watched Bess nervously, still wiping the table with the cloth. It was getting an extra polish.

Another door opened, and Bess turned to see a huge woman. She had trouble getting through the door frame, but once she was in the room, she looked very agile on her feet. Based on the apron around her waist, Bess figured she was the innkeeper's wife. She shot her husband a black look and then hurried to Bess. "Of course, sir," she said sweetly. "We also have some local beer and some very good sausages. And the hay and water for the horses goes without saying," she added with a wave of her hand. She smiled brightly at Bess and winked. Bess felt a little restless around her. He looked over his shoulder at the coach, but Finn was still checking the wheels. Bess wished Finn had already come inside.

"We have some potatoes and milk for the coachman," the innkeeper's wife said, looking at Finn, too.

"I think he needs something more nourishing than that," Bess said with a smile. "Something with a lot of meat. The price isn't an issue," he added. The innkeeper's wife looked at him with a bright smile. Her husband still polished the table, watching the conversation.

"It's very noble of you," the woman said. "Most people try to get their coachmen the cheapest offering. One guy even ordered only potatoes. He said that we weren't to bother with butter. Do you remember?" She turned to her husband. The innkeeper straightened up and nodded. He looked down at the table again, and when he spotted a polished circle in the centre, he blushed.

"I'll take care of the horses," the woman said and meaningfully looked at her husband. The innkeeper looked at his wife and then turned to Bess with a wooden smile. The woman left the inn.

"Please, sit down," the innkeeper said to Bess, and he motioned to the table by the window. "Do you want anything to drink?"

"Two pints of beer, please," Bess said as he walked to the table.

He sat down at the table and watched the innkeeper, who walked behind the counter and started to pour beer into a big glass. Bess looked out of the window. The coach was taking up most of the space in front of the inn, blocking the view. Bess was glad. He was curious about the people in the city, but it seemed that the people were more curious about him. He didn't want to feel as if he was on display.

Finn and the innkeeper's wife were nowhere to be seen. Bess leaned towards the window, looking for the Finn by the horses. He still couldn't' see him anywhere. Suddenly, Finn stepped into Bess's view, carrying two buckets of water. He placed the buckets in front of the horses and brushed off his hands. The horses immediately stooped down and started to drink.

Bess looked around, curious to know where the beer was. There was a half-full glass on the bar with fallen foam, and the innkeeper was gone. The hair on Bess's neck stood up. He slowly rose in his seat, ready to flee, but just then, the innkeeper stood up from behind the counter with a wet cloth in his hands. Bess relaxed and sat back down. The innkeeper threw the cloth to the corner and picked up the glass from the counter. Looking at the barrel, he continued pouring beer into the glass.

The door of the inn opened, and Finn entered. He was wiping his hands with a cloth, looking down. He lifted his gaze, which immediately fell on the beer in the innkeeper's hands. He stopped in the middle of the room and licked his lips, not taking his eyes off the glass. Bess coughed, and Finn looked around with start. When he noticed Bess by the window, he stepped towards him, watching the innkeeper over his shoulder. He sat down, still not taking his eyes off the beer in the innkeeper's hands.

The innkeeper's wife returned to the inn and, with surprising speed, walked through the room. She vanished through the door on the other side while the innkeeper drew the second beer. Bess looked out of the window. The horses now also had hay in front of them. They both looked very content at the moment.

The innkeeper's wife returned quickly, carrying a plate. She put it on the bar and vanished through the door again. The innkeeper picked up the two pints of beers in one hand and the big plate in the other and brought it all to their table. A wide smile appeared on Finn's face as he spotted the selection of meat and cheeses.

"This is our specialty," the innkeeper said.

"Do you get many travellers here?" Bess asked as he took a piece of cheese from the plate and took a bite. It was tasty. He motioned for Finn to eat, and he turned to the innkeeper.

"Not really, no," the innkeeper said nervously. "Just about three weeks ago, we got this strange guy here. He was very tall and had the greenest eyes you ever saw."

Bess froze with another piece of cheese in his hand. He looked at the innkeeper. It seemed that the innkeeper was keen on discussing the strange visitor. Most likely he would also discuss Bess's visit with other visitors too, but that didn't bother Bess at the moment.

"Really?" he asked as he put another piece of cheese into his mouth. It melted on his tongue. "Did he mention anything interesting?"

"He was looking for someone," the innkeeper said. "He didn't know the exact description, but he said that it was someone like him. He said that I would remember him because of his very blue eyes. He said that there would be something weird about the person. It was a strange statement, since his eyes looked like they were shining." After this, the innkeeper looked Bess deep in the eye. Bess understood immediately that he was checking to see what colour Bess's eyes were. When the innkeeper saw that they were brown, he looked a little disappointed.

"Have you seen anyone like that?" Bess asked curiously.

The innkeeper shook his head sadly. "As I said, we don't get many visitors. We have two rooms here, but they are usually empty. Our main business is food."

"It's very delicious," Finn said with his mouth full of meat. Bess looked down. Half of the food that had been on the plate was already gone. He pushed the plate closer to Finn, whose eyes shone with excitement.

"How long did the man stay?" Bess asked, and he took a sip from his beer.

"Just a few hours," the innkeeper said. At that moment, his wife returned to the room. The innkeeper smiled at Bess and Finn and walked back to the bar. Bess didn't need any more answers, so he let him. He turned to the plate and watched the last piece of meat vanish into Finn's mouth.

In silence, Bess drank his beer, thinking about Rex. It seemed that Rex was looking for someone like him. Three weeks ago. That was before they had met in the mines. Bess looked at Finn, who was gulping his beer. He put the half-drunk glass down and wiped his mouth with the back of his hand. Bess leaned in. "Have you heard anything since we arrived?" he asked him.

Finn thought about this and then shook his head. He picked up the last piece of cheese and ate it. Bess sighed. "Maybe we'll find out more when we get to the fortress," Finn said. He picked up his glass and finished his beer.

Bess nodded absentmindedly.

Ethan sat in his office reading a report from Captain Stuart. It turned out that Bess had mostly read the kings' diaries when he was in Norene. Ethan wondered how much information Bess could have gleaned from those books.

He put aside the report and picked up Lord Thomas's report on the state of the troops by the borders. The Royal Guards were now patrolling the borders, replacing the soldiers who had formerly been Lord Blake's. Ethan wondered about the army. Should he put everything into the Royal Guards, or should he split the chores? The Royal Guards were more like protectors of the people of Norene and the king; the soldiers were guarding the borders and seas. Maybe he could create two divisions of Royal Guards—the Royal Guards and the—

Lord Adrian entered the office and broke Ethan's chain of thoughts. Ethan put the report down and rubbed his eyes. Lord Adrian closed the door behind him and stepped to the desk. "I have some good news, Your Majesty," he said with a smile. Ethan looked up at him. "Lord Charles with his wife, daughter, and Daniel have arrived."

"That's really good news," Ethan said and stood up. "I've been looking forward to seeing Daniel again. Though I wish that they'd come when I still had that necklace he gave me."

"He might be able to find it," Lord Adrian suggested as he opened the door for Ethan. "His sense of smell should be better than ours, I believe."

"Sometimes I'm not sure whether you're kidding or you're serious," Ethan said with a smile, and he walked outside the office.

Lord Adrian chuckled. They walked down the corridor, Lord Adrian leading the way. "I ordered the servants to prepare the spare rooms on the third floor," Lord Adrian said over his shoulder as they reached the stairs. "There are three adjoining rooms. Lucy is getting married, and she and her mother want to go to the city to buy some dresses and stuff. I ordered a coach to be ready for them for tomorrow."

"Did Lucy's future husband come? I'm rather curious about the man. I assume it's not Daniel," he said and paused. "Or is it?"

"I asked Lord Charles the same question," Lord Adrian said with a chuckle. "He looked annoyed by the question. He said that she's marrying a boy from their town. I believe she knows him from her childhood. And he didn't come, just the family."

They reached the door to a room that was right beneath Lady Joan's quarters and stepped inside. It was a spacious anteroom with three chairs and a sofa around a small table. There was a door on each wall, one of which led to a small balcony. Lord Charles sat by the table. He jumped up from his chair as soon as they entered and hurried towards Ethan. "Your Majesty," he said with a little bow of his head.

"I'm glad you came to visit us," Ethan said with a smile. The door to his left opened, and two women entered, looking rather nervous. "I believe that this is your lovely family."

"Yes," Lord Charles said quickly, motioning for Lucy and Mary to approach them. "This is my wonderful wife, Mary, and this is our daughter, Lucy."

Mary was completely flushed, and she bowed deeply when Lord Charles introduced her. Lucy bowed to Ethan too. She looked slightly nervous but otherwise unmoved by Ethan's presence. Ethan immediately noticed many similarities between Lord Charles and Lucy. Her hair was the same colour, she had the same smile, and she had the same twinkle in her eyes. She was pretty and seemed nice. Ethan didn't wonder at all why she had become engaged at such a young age.

"I hope you will enjoy your stay," Ethan said to them. "Daniel didn't come with you?"

Lord Charles looked around as if expecting Daniel to appear in the corner. There were some voices in the corridor, but otherwise the place was quiet. He hesitated and then spun around again, still checking the room. "He might have gotten lost," Lord Charles said nervously. "He was with us when we arrived."

At that moment, Lord James entered the room with Daniel walking by his side. Lord James had a wide smile on his lips as he listened to Daniel's monologue: "… but she was mad at me for jumping up there. And then Charles said that's what people do. I can tell you that wolves don't behave like that at all. It really doesn't make any sense, does it? I never saw you behave like that with Lord Adrian, or anyone else."

"Your Majesty," said Lord James to Ethan with a bow. He had a wide smile on his face, though he also looked slightly embarrassed. Daniel followed Lord James's stare and brightened up when he spotted Ethan.

"Hi, Daniel," Ethan said with a smile.

Daniel jumped in the air with delight, and in three more jumps approached Ethan. He threw his arms around Ethan's neck and hugged him. Lord James burst out laughing. Lord Charles went pale and reached towards Daniel. He pulled him back, meeting Ethan's stare for a moment.

Ethan had been surprised by Daniel's affection, too, but quickly beckoned for the others to relax. It was nice to have someone so happy to see him. He would never expect Daniel to know proper etiquette. It was rather refreshing that he didn't.

"Glad to see you too," Ethan said with a smile as he patted Daniel's shoulder.

"It's great to be here," Daniel said breathlessly. He hadn't noticed anything odd about the situation. "I couldn't wait to get here! I'm so glad that you invited us."

"I'm glad you all came," Ethan said as he looked around the room. Lord Adrian's eyes were round with surprise, and he had an uncertain smile on his lips. Lord James had tears in his eyes and was silently laughing. Lord Charles was pale, smiling nervously. He was still holding Daniel's shoulder, watching Ethan. Mary stood behind Lord Charles, watching the scene, her mouth covered with her hand. Her eyes were round with shock. Lucy had also covered her mouth and her eyes were also closed, and she was shaking slightly.

Ethan turned to Lord Charles. "You missed the ball," he said. "But you didn't miss much."

"Except an attack on our king," Lord James added, wiping a tear out of his eye. Mary and Lucy gasped, and Lord Charles's eyes went round. Daniel looked in surprise from Lord James to Ethan.

"It's not even worth mentioning," Ethan said, waving his hand dismissively. "I would rather talk about something more interesting. Maybe we could have some small entertainment in the castle—a masquerade, perhaps; with just the residents of the castle and Lord Thomas. I believe he's still staying in the city."

He looked at Lord James. There was a smug smile on his face. It was clear that Lord James understood Ethan's motives for the masquerade all too well. Ethan didn't mind. The truth was that he wanted to host a small social gathering so he could get to know Lady Joan, but he also wanted Lord Charles and his family feel welcome in the castle. Though getting to know Lady Joan was the stronger motivation.

"Yes, Lord Thomas is still here," Lord Adrian said. "He claims that he needs to make sure that the rotation of the guards to the borders is in order."

"I think that he will go on diet once he gets back home," Lord James said with a snigger. "Maybe he wants to postpone that, and that's why he's still here."

Ethan smiled. "I don't think that being this long away from his family does him any good," he said. Lord James chuckled.

"I will send him an invitation right away," Lord Adrian said. "It will at least give him an excuse to stay a little longer."

Ethan smiled and turned to Lord Charles. "I hope you will join us," Ethan said to him. Mary nodded happily and glanced at her daughter. There was a strange excitement in her posture. Lucy didn't seem to be very impressed with the invitation.

"I'd like to talk to you, Daniel," Ethan said as he turned to Daniel. "Would you like to go for a little walk around the castle?"

Daniel jumped with excitement and nodded vigorously. Lord James got a coughing fit and quickly left the quarters. Ethan nodded to others and left the room. Daniel hurried after Ethan, skipping by his side.

Ethan wanted to tell Daniel about the necklace but seeing Daniel so happy made it difficult. He didn't want to disappoint him. They walked in silence for a while, and then Ethan decided to start on a safer topic. He didn't want to deliver the bad news so quickly. "Will you come to the masquerade too?" he asked, turning to Daniel.

Daniel stopped skipping and thought for a moment, walking calmly by Ethan's side. Then he shrugged. "I'm not sure what a masquerade is, but I'll join you," he said.

"A masquerade is a gathering with dances and food, but the visitors have to wear masks. We have some masks stored away somewhere here in the castle. You can choose whichever one you like."

"Why would you do that?"

Ethan was surprised at Daniel's question, and he watched Daniel intently. "Because I consider you my friend?" Ethan ventured.

"But why a mask? Why dance and eat … Okay, I understand the eating part," Daniel corrected himself.

"Oh, you mean why a masquerade." Ethan laughed. "It's a human thing. We also like to use gatherings like those to meet other people."

"Can't you just meet them?"

Ethan had no idea what to say to that. "Yes," he said slowly. "But this way we have time to get to know each other and enjoy that time together … " His voice trailed off.

"But why?"

Ethan sighed. He wasn't ready to answer such difficult questions about basic things.

Suddenly, Daniel stopped and sniffed the air. Ethan stopped too and looked around, surprised. Daniel sniffed the air some more and spun around. "Where is the necklace?" Daniel asked, and he turned to Ethan.

Ethan sighed and rubbed the bridge of his nose. "That's what I wanted to talk to you about. I lost it," Ethan admitted. "I keep looking for it, but I can't find it anywhere. I'm really sorry. I hope you can help me find it."

Daniel sniffed the air again. He looked at the ceiling. He stepped away from Ethan, sniffing loudly. "I can smell it," he said. "It was here, but I don't know how long ago." He walked to the corner, followed by Ethan. "Someone had to find it and take it away," Daniel said, sniffing. Then he stopped on the spot and spun around, looking surprised.

"What's wrong?"

"It's gone," Daniel said with dismay. "The trail just vanished! It was here a moment ago!"

A guard walked pass them. He saluted to Ethan and turned the corner. Even Ethan could smell the guard who was sweating a lot. Daniel wriggled his nose.

"It's really gone," he said sadly as he stepped towards Ethan. "But it was here for sure; and not with your scent. This is maybe the place where you lost it. Looks like someone else found it. Maybe I can find the trail elsewhere," Daniel added and sniffed the air. He hurried down the corridor, leaving Ethan behind.

"Just don't change, okay?" Ethan called after him. He hesitated for a moment, wondering if it would be better for him to run after Daniel. Before he could make the decision, he heard footsteps. He spun around, expecting to see a guard, but he was surprised to see Lady Joan. As soon as she turned the corner and spotted Ethan, she smiled at him.

"I was just going for a walk … Ethan," she said a little shyly.

"That's a wonderful idea," Ethan said in a higher voice than usual. He cleared his throat and put his hands behind his back. "Would you like some company?" he said lowering his voice too much.

"I'd love some," Lady Joan replied.

Ethan offered her his arm. Thrill ran through him as she touched him. They stepped along the corridor in silence, Ethan quickly going through all possible topics of conversation. "There will be a masquerade here soon," he said. "I hope you will join us. It'll be just a small gathering. Lord Charles came with his family and a friend, Lord Thomas will probably join us from the city, so will Lords James and Adrian."

"I'll feel so strange among so many well-bred gentlemen," Lady Joan confessed, and she turned red. "I wouldn't know what to talk about."

"Small talk is always safe. Besides, Lord Charles hasn't been a lord for long, though I'm glad I met him. His wife seems lovely, and they have a daughter who's getting married soon."

"Do you like small talk?" Lady Joan asked Ethan.

"No. But one of the privileges of being king is to have meaningful conversations," he admitted. "You can always pretend that you're too busy for small talk. My father used that excuse a lot: 'Don't let me detain you.' Of course, it meant that he didn't want to waste their time, which was a polite way of saying that he didn't want them to waste his. But it sometimes made people unsure if he perhaps meant to lock them up. No one ever asked; they just bowed and quickly left him alone."

"That's actually mean," Lady Joan said with a merry laugh. "Yet brilliant! Unfortunately, I don't have any authority to detain people literally, so I can't use this excuse. Do you use it?"

Ethan laughed and shook his head. They reached the stairs and started their descent. "I'm still getting used to this. It all changed so fast. Sometimes I feel like a little boy, unsure what to do or how to act. I'm trying to remember my teachings, and I read books on laws and etiquette over and over again. But I miss my father. He ruled for over two decades, and people really loved him. I was too young to understand that I should have used every moment to not only listen to his advice, but to remember it all."

"You're a very good king," Lady Joan said encouragingly. "People love you already. There aren't a lot of kings who have to fight for their throne the first week of their reign. Yet you won and even made truce with Wolfast."

"Sounds good when you say it like that," Ethan said. He felt light as a feather knowing that Lady Joan thought he was a good king. At that moment, he wanted to be the best king of Norene ever!

They turned another corner and stepped onto the castle yard. Ethan immediately spotted Daniel in the yard, sitting on the tiles and sniffing a piece of wood. Ethan quickly steered Lady Joan to the other side, hoping that she hadn't noticed anything. Lady Joan gently pushed him towards the gate. Ethan really wanted to go outside and have a nice long walk, but two things stopped him: Daniel probably needed some looking after before he did something stupid, and Ethan had made a promise to Lord James that he wouldn't leave the castle without letting him know in advance.

"I have some duties to attend to," he told Lady Joan. "Thank you for the short walk. Sometime soon we should take some horses and ride through the forests."

"It would be my pleasure, Sire," Lady Joan said with a bow as she let go of his arm.

Ethan wanted to remind her to call him Ethan, but then he noticed Captain Stuart standing nearby, waiting for an opportunity to talk to him. Ethan smiled at Lady Joan and bowed his head. When she walked through the gate, he turned to Captain Stuart. "Is there something urgent, Captain?" Ethan asked calmly.

Captain Stuart limped to Ethan and looked at Daniel, who was standing by the walls with another piece of wood in his hand. Daniel sniffed the wood and tasted it. "No, Your Majesty," Captain Stuart said and turned back to Ethan. "I just wanted to inquire about Daniel. I understand that he's not a real werewolf, but the servants and the guards might get nervous."

Ethan scanned the yard. The guards were indeed watching Daniel, who was now walking slowly by the wall bent double, scanning the ground. Daniel unfortunately chose that moment to fall on all four and sniff the ground. The guards laughed. Daniel either didn't notice that or chose to ignore it. He stood up, brushed his hands against his trousers, and continued.

Ethan pressed his lips together. He didn't like the laughter of the guards. "I will talk to him," he said to the captain. "I want to make it absolutely clear that he's my guest and friend. He's not to be harmed in any way."

"He will be treated nicely here, Sire. I will personally see to that," Captain Stuart said with a small bow of his head.

Ethan looked at the captain and nodded. That was enough for Ethan. He turned around and walked towards Daniel, who sat down on the ground. When Ethan was a few steps away from Daniel, Daniel looked up. The moment he spotted Ethan, a wide smile appeared on his face. "I think I figured it out," he said proudly.

Ethan frowned for a moment, not sure what Daniel was talking about, but then he put the pieces together. "You found the necklace?"

"No, but I know why I can't smell it. Someone took it and put it into a box or a bag. If I can find the box or the bag, I will find the necklace."

"How can you find the container? The castle's big and there are many rooms. And the necklace might have left the castle already."

"What's a container?" Daniel asked, tilting his head to one side.

Ethan froze, watching Daniel intently. It was strange that Daniel, who had been able to comprehend so much so fast in the past, was suddenly asking so many questions.

"It's something you use to put stuff in," Ethan said, wondering if he should carry a dictionary with him. "Like a bag or a box. There's one word for all of them."

"Oh," Daniel said.

"And as I was saying, the necklace could have left the castle already."

"I don't think so," Daniel said thoughtfully. "I don't know why, but it feels as if it's still here—as if the castle is filled with its presence."

Ethan looked up at the castle walls and slowly nodded. He didn't know how else to put it. He had a strong suspicion that the necklace was still inside. It was as if it was calling to him; if only he knew how to follow that call.

"Before you go around looking for it," Ethan said, turning to Daniel, "please, bear in mind that these people don't like werewolves. So try to look more like a human. Also, if you change back and forth, they might take you for a werewolf and might try to harm you. Please, don't place yourself in that danger."

Daniel looked up at Ethan with a surprised look, and then a smile brightened his face. Once again, he reminded Ethan of a puppy. There was something incredibly doglike about him. "I promise you I won't," Daniel said. Suddenly, he yawned and rubbed his eyes.

"You had a long drive here, and it's getting late," Ethan said, and he motioned for Daniel to follow him. "Maybe you should go back to your quarters and take a rest."

"Quarters?" Daniel asked and stood up.

"Your room," Ethan explained, looking sideways at Daniel. Daniel yawned and nodded.

Chapter 3

Bess sat in the coach, reading a book. The drive was long and boring, and reading books was the only pastime he had. However, after several hours of travel, he was getting tired of books. He put the book aside and rubbed his eyes. Suddenly, the coach slowed down and then came to a complete halt. Bess leaned towards the window, surprised. They were in the middle of the forest. There were trees everywhere around them. A river roared in the distance. The coach door suddenly opened, and Finn stepped into the view. Bess frowned at him. "We're here?"

"Yes," Finn said, and he motioned over his shoulder into the forest. Bess couldn't see much in that direction. "We can't continue with the coach from here because the path leading up to the fortress is not wide enough. Even the horses couldn't climb it on their own," he added. "This was built as a secure fortress, and it's very difficult to reach the top. But I'm sure you can climb it without any trouble. You had a great physique even before you became a werewolf. I can help you with your things if you want." Finn motioned towards the bag that contained Bess's clothes and books.

"That's all right," Bess said as he stepped out of the coach. He pulled his bag closer and opened it. "I won't need all of this up there," he said to Finn as he pulled a small pouch of money out. "Go back to the village we passed an hour ago and wait for me there. Here's enough money for the inn." He gave Finn the pouch. "The innkeeper mentioned that they have two rooms there, so you shouldn't have too much trouble. You can read my books while I'm away."

Finn took the money and doubtfully looked at the book in the coach. "I'll come back as soon as I'm done here," Bess said, and he stepped away from the coach. He looked around. There was a narrow and steep path nearby. It had to lead to the fortress. Bess was curious about the setup. There were supposed to be guards at the fortress, and they needed food. Maybe part of the guards' duties was carrying food uphill.

Finn closed the coach door behind Bess, making Bess jump with a start. Finn jumped up onto the driver's seat, took the reins, and turned in the seat. Then he looked down at Bess and froze. "Should I come and check on you sometime?" he asked.

Bess looked at the path again and pressed his lips together. "No need," he said as he turned to Finn. "If something happens, I know where to find you."

Finn nodded. "Good luck," he said with a small bow of his head, and he urged the horses to move along. Bess stepped back to get out of the range of flying stones and watched Finn leave. He watched until the coach vanished into the forest. Then he turned to the path in the forest and started to climb the hill. He wasn't sure if Finn had found the correct path because this one was awfully steep. It was one of the steepest hills Bess had ever climbed. There was no way that food could have been carried up there along this path. He was a werewolf, and even he was having trouble climbing the rock. Maybe it was a shortcut.

After half an hour, he had to stop to catch his breath. His self-confidence had been seriously damaged by the climb. If the guards could actually climb this, then he was doing something wrong. Maybe the guards in the fortress created a chain and passed packages of food from one man to the next. He was becoming curious about this arrangement. He had to acknowledge that the fortress was well protected. There was no way that an army could approach this place.

Once he caught his breath, he continued his climb. After a few minutes, he finally reached the top, and a tall building appeared in front of him. It was five stories high, and he noticed some gargoyles beneath the roof. Bess couldn't see too much from the entrance because part of the building was hidden by the forest. The rest of the area was rock. In the distance, he heard the river.

He stopped for a moment to catch his breath and then continued to the main gate. The gate was two stories high and looked very solid. He half expected to see a man with a bow aiming at him from a window on a higher floor, but the place looked deserted. He banged on the wood three times and waited. After a while, the gate opened with strange clicking sound. Bess watched the dark entrance, not seeing anyone there. The gate stopped moving, leaving enough space for one person to enter.

A moment later, a young man stepped outside. He looked Bess up and down. "Good morning, sir," the man said. It seemed he knew who Bess was. He motioned for Bess to enter, stepping inside. Bess walked through the entrance, glancing at a bright yard in front of him. "Do you have any luggage, sir?"

"No," Bess said, and he stopped at the beginning of the yard. The guard shrugged and turned to the gate. Bess heard the gate close with the same clicking sound. He didn't look at the gate. Instead, he watched an older round man, probably the owner, hurry to him through the yard. "Good morning," Bess said when the man finally reached him, completely out of breath.

"Good … morning … sir," the man said, fighting for breath. "I've been … expecting you … later."

"We had a very uneventful ride," Bess said conversantly. "I won't take much of your time, though. I just need to see your library."

"I understand." The man nodded and placed his palms on his knees, bending down. Bess patiently waited for him to catch his breath. A few seconds later, the man straightened up and turned towards the nearest door. He was red in the face. "The letter you sent was very clear on the instructions," he said, and he motioned for Bess to follow. "We have kept records here since the fortress was built," the man said proudly. "I'm Herbert. If you need anything, just let me know."

"That's great. Thank you," Bess said with a smile as he followed Herbert into the building. "The only thing I need right now is your library. Oh, and has someone rather strange been here recently? In the past few months?"

"Strange?" Herbert said, obviously thinking about the question. "We had a thief here. Awful business. The guard who found the thief nearly died. And then the guards spoke of a shadow in the fortress. They thought it was the ghost of some guard who had died a long time ago and was trying to warn them. You know the guards," he said with a laugh. "They believe anything that makes this work more thrilling. Or as my dad used to say, anything that makes it harder."

"What happened to the ghost?" Bess asked, curiosity rising inside him. He had a hunch that the ghost was someone real—maybe the woman that he saw with Rex or the person Rex was looking for when he was in Wolfast. This was no coincidence.

"I don't think there ever was one," Herbert said, seeming to be a little annoyed. "It was just their imagination."

"When did the ghost arrive?"

"I told you it wasn't real!"

"Sorry," Bess said with an apologetic smile. "I meant to ask when the guards first mentioned this superstition."

"Oh, I don't know," Herbert said impatiently. "Soon after the theft, but it lasted only a few days. When I wanted proof, they claimed they couldn't see him anymore. As I said, the ghost wasn't real."

"You wrote to the capital regarding the theft," Bess continued. Herbert nodded vigorously. "Did you do—I mean … What else did you do regarding this situation?"

"Not much," Herbert said with a shrug. "My great-grandfather got a small necklace to use when this sort of thing happens. It was a gift from a stranger. It was passed to me by my father. He told me to use it if something odd happened, but when I did, nothing happened. Only the guards got paranoid and said that there was a ghost in the fortress."

They reached a big door, and Herbert pushed it open. As it creaked open, stale air reached Bess's nose. He could smell parchment, but also dust and probably a mould. Luckily, he wasn't planning on staying too long.

"I can try to find that necklace if you want it," Herbert said to Bess, but Bess just shook his head.

"I'm not interested in the necklace. I just wish to know if you were supposed to use it in case of theft in general or—"

"No, only if the object hidden in room four-oh-five got stolen," Herbert said. Bess nodded. "Can I bring you something?" Herbert asked politely. Bess believed the man hoped the answer would be no.

"Some light for reading, please," Bess said, looking into the darkness. Herbert looked disappointed. "And maybe something to drink," Bess added as an afterthought.

Christine wanted to get some sleep, but she was so angry over John's reaction that she couldn't even close her eyes. She paced her flat for an hour and then decided to go to work. When she arrived, she saw that John was already behind his table, drawing something. He looked up from the paper, and when he spotted Christine, he quickly looked down. There was hardly an audible greeting from him.

Unfortunately, John had already informed Edmund that Christine wouldn't be in that day. What was worse, John had told Edmund the reason why—her night visit to the old warehouse. That day at work turned out to be one of the worst. John was very quiet and barely answered anyone's questions, let alone Christine's, and Edmund was mad because Christine had gone out the previous night and risked everything, starting with the good word Edmund had put in for her with Captain Stuart and ending with her life. On top of it, she was very tired from the lack of sleep and therefore annoyed with John, Edmund, and the world in general. Her colleagues tried to cheer her up. On the one hand, she was grateful that they cared for her, but on the other, she would have been happier to be left alone.

She left The Royal Printer very early, slamming the door behind her. She knew that her early departure, not to mention her theatrical flair, would earn her a meeting with Edmund the next day, but at the moment she didn't care. She would have slammed the gate as well, but it was way too heavy.

She decided to get something done. She wasn't going to just wait for Rex to win. She wasn't sure how to get an audience with the king, but she knew where to ask. A few minutes later, she entered the headquarters of the Royal Guards and stopped by the front desk. A guard was sitting behind the counter reading a report of some kind. Christine stopped in front of him and waited. When he didn't react, she coughed. The guard looked up. When he spotted her, he stood up. "Good morning, ma'am," he said. "How may I be of service?"

"I would like to get an audience with the king. Can you advise me where I can do this?"

The guard's eyes went round. "Audience?" He looked around as if looking for someone with higher seniority or more experience. "Could you please wait here?" he asked and left before Christine could reply.

Christine paced the room, waiting for the guard to return. A few guards came and went, all of them looking at Christine curiously. Five minutes later, Christine wondered if she should just leave. Maybe she needed to travel all the way to the castle to request an audience. Maybe she could have gone to Lord Thomas's palace. Lord Thomas might be there.

Just as she decided to leave the building, the guard returned to the room and stopped by the desk. "There is a waiting list for the king, ma'am," he said. "If you want, I can write down your name, and if the king decides to give you an audience, we can contact you."

"How long will it take?"

"I don't know," the guard said with an apologetic smile. "The king isn't giving any audiences at the moment. The list already contains about a hundred names. Because of this business with the Masked Man, Captain Stuart and Lord James decided to postpone the audiences. Once the Masked Man is under lock and key, the king will gladly see you."

"Thank you," Christine said, feeling disappointed.

"Should I add your name to the list?" the guard asked her as he picked up a piece of paper. "I will need your name, your father's name, and your address. And, of course, information about the purpose of the audience."

"No need," Christine said with a forced smile. "I will check with you in a few days if I still want the audience."

The guard smiled at her and nodded. He put the paper aside and sat down. "Is there anything else I can do for you?" he asked.

For a moment Christine thought of requesting a meeting with Captain Stuart, but she changed her mind. She was in no mood to talk to the captain. He probably already knew about Rex anyway. "No, thank you," she said in whisper, her voice giving temporarily up.

The guard looked at Christine and hesitated. She got the impression that he wanted to say something. She decided to leave before he could. She smiled at him, spun around, and left the building. At the threshold, she looked back at the guard who was reading the report once again.

She closed the door and stepped onto the pavement. There she took a deep breath. Anger filled her once again. John was acting weird, Edmund was mad at her, and her plan for meeting the king hadn't worked.

Still fuming, she went home where she paced for nearly two hours until she calmed down. Suddenly, her plan to meet the king seemed farfetched. She had always known that in her heart, but that morning she had felt hope. She'd had a feeling she could do it. Now she felt furious and discouraged. No one was helping her with this. She wanted to talk to the king, but she was very unlikely to get past his lords or Captain Stuart. Maybe there was some plot to keep the king uninformed. That sounded like something Captain Stuart might support.

As soon as she thought of Captain Stuart, she realized that he would never let her talk to the king without finding out why she wanted to in the first place. She didn't like the option of talking to Captain Stuart about the Masked Man. He wouldn't understand and might even laugh at her. And if he was in a plot with Rex, he would definitely keep her away from the king. She might even be in danger from him.

She needed to talk to someone about this. John knew a lot, but he was acting weird, like the little field boy he was. The possibility that he might be scared wasn't a valid excuse for Christine. She'd had the shit scared out of her, but she kept on going. She wasn't scared of the Masked Man anymore, but she wasn't sure how to tell him that Rex was in the city. She had to find him, that was certain. Now the question was how. There wasn't any other option; she would have to go outside and search for him the old-fashioned way.

She was so mad at John and everyone that she had no trouble staying awake until night fell. Completely ignoring Edmund's reproaches about risking her life, she walked outside. It was a very dark night as the sky was covered with clouds. She wasn't scared; rather, she was excited. She felt so alive and active. This was better than sitting at home and biting her nails.

After an hour, she was rather disappointed; two more hours later, she was angry; and after another hour, she gave up and went home. The city had been flooded with the Royal Guards. They were on every corner and had watched her suspiciously. When she walked towards an alleyway, they followed her, asking if she was lost. There was no chance of meeting the Masked Man anywhere in the city that night. If he as much as showed his shadow anywhere, there would be too many guards on top of him.

She lay in her bed and looked at the ceiling, fuming. The old-fashioned way wasn't good enough. She needed some other way of communicating with the Masked Man, though she had no idea how to achieve this. It was very late at night when she finally fell asleep, and she had weird dreams of falling roofs and shadows chasing her through streets.

The next morning, Ethan stepped out of his quarters and slowly walked towards the stairs. A few guards patrolled the corridor and nervously saluted him. He reached the staircase and had descended halfway when he spotted something white and furry turn the corner. He stopped and frowned. There weren't any dogs inside the castle; therefore, he came to the first possible conclusion that came to his mind.

He hurried after the apparition and stopped in the middle of the corridor. Daniel, in his white-wolf form, walked along the corridor slowly, sniffing every inch of the floor. Ethan followed him, moving his feet slowly forward. He walked past a window, and a warm summer breeze washed around him. Daniel stopped, lifted his head, and sniffed the air. Then he looked over his shoulder. The moment he spotted Ethan, he froze. His eyes went round, creating an adorable puppy look on his face.

"May I ask what're you doing?" Ethan said, folding his arms. Daniel's ears moved back. He lowered his head, still looking up at Ethan. "Didn't I ask you not to draw attention to yourself?" Ethan snapped.

Daniel tilted his head to left and flipped his ears up. Ethan took this to mean: "What?" Ethan sighed and looked up and down the corridor. Luckily, they were still alone. Daniel straightened up and turned towards Ethan. He sat down and watched Ethan curiously.

"Do you understand that people in Norene aren't currently friendly towards werewolves?" Ethan asked in a kindlier tone. Daniel nodded. It felt weird to talk to a wolf, but the fact the wolf answered was even weirder. "And do you understand that a wolf who can understand people would be treated as a werewolf?" Daniel once again tilted his head to left. Ethan sighed. "Maybe we should have this conversation in private," he said, and he motioned for Daniel to follow him.

Daniel stood up and trotted behind Ethan, his head hung low. Ethan looked over his shoulder at Daniel, and his heart melted. Instinctively, as if dealing with a dog, he slowed down and patted Daniel on his head. Daniel looked up. He seemed surprised, and he wagged his tail.

31

"I'm not angry," Ethan said, and Daniel's tail started to move even faster. "I'm just worried that something might happen to you." Out of the corner of his eye, Ethan noticed a guard. The guard was watching them with his mouth gaping open. He quickly collected himself and saluted. Ethan ignored him.

Ethan returned to his quarters with Daniel at his side. He opened the door for Daniel and watched him enter the anteroom with his head hung low. Ethan couldn't stay angry at Daniel. With a sigh, he entered too and closed the door. Daniel sat down in the middle of the room, looking sad. Ethan walked around him towards the cabinet that held a basin and a jug of water. He grabbed the cloth on the table and took it to Daniel. He held it in front of him and then looked at Daniel.

"Use this to cover yourself up after you change," he said as kindly as he could, and he turned towards the window. He remembered the moment when he'd first seen the beginning of Daniel's transformation, and he was in no mood to witness the full thing.

There was a strange sound behind him, and then Daniel said sheepishly: "Done."

Ethan spun around to see Daniel in front of him with the cloth tied around his waist and a nervous look on his face. Ethan wanted to snap at Daniel for walking the corridors like a wolf, but he couldn't bring himself to do it. He felt like a monster attacking a puppy for being too small. "I should have some extra clothes here," Ethan said as he walked towards the wardrobe. Usually, the servants prepared his clothes for him in the morning. He dressed himself, but he never had to choose what to wear. Therefore, he wasn't sure where his clothes were stored. He opened the first wardrobe and stopped in surprise. He had discovered a small private armoury packed with swords, crossbows, shields, and daggers.

"Huh!" he said. He picked up a sword. It was not a fancy sword, yet it looked sturdy. He put it back and closed the wardrobe, moving to the one next to it. It contained a small library. Ethan didn't think that any books had been stored in his quarters. He always went to the library and chose a book of his liking. These books had been his father's. He recognized a book on tactics which his father used to read a lot when Ethan was a boy. Ethan had liked the book because of the all the diagrams of battlefields.

"I have never really checked these," he said to Daniel as he closed the wardrobe. "I thought when I moved here that all these wardrobes contained only clothes."

"I have only two pairs of trousers and three shirts," Daniel said with a shrug. "Charles gave them to me. He wanted to give me more, but I don't see what's so important about clothes."

"They keep us warm," Ethan said. He knew that there was no point in explaining about decency. Wolves wore no clothes. "Now you will have one more of each," he added. He opened the last wardrobe and finally found his clothes. He picked up one pair of trousers and one shirt and turned to Daniel. Daniel threw the cloth onto the floor and then took the clothes from Ethan. He put them on. Both the shirt and the trousers fit to perfection.

"These are comfortable," Daniel said as he tied the belt on the trousers.

"Well, these weren't cheap," Ethan said with a smile, and he closed the wardrobe door.

"You paid for these?" Daniel asked stupefied.

Ethan opened his mouth to answer and then decided to let it be. "Okay," he said, "tell me what you were doing in that corridor."

"I was looking for the necklace," Daniel said in a matter-of-fact tone of voice. He looked around the room, looking at the walls with interest.

"I told you not to walk around as a wolf, didn't I?"

"No, you said that people were nervous about werewolves, so I thought that I shouldn't change in public," Daniel said calmly. He leaned his head way back and checked the ceiling. "That could make them nervous. Though people in Charles's palace were very nice about that. They even gave me some ham whenever I came to the kitchen. And when I changed and attacked Lucy's fiancé, they actually laughed about it. So I thought that you didn't want the people here to see me change. I understand that it's not a pretty sight."

"Hold on, hold on," Ethan said and rubbed the bridge of his nose. "You attacked Lucy's fiancé?"

Daniel looked at Ethan, furrows appearing on his forehead. "Why does everyone find that interesting?" he asked. Then he relaxed. "I didn't know that he was her fiancé at the time. I thought he was attacking her, so I jumped at him. Obviously, they were … *kissing*. I have no idea what that is," Daniel confessed. "Do you know why people kiss?"

"Ehm … " Ethan said, blood rushing to his cheeks. "Here, people aren't so friendly towards werewolves," he said, deciding to ignore Daniel's question. "You see, they have experienced the real werewolves, the ones that are really aggressive and dangerous, not the nice ones. So any wolf that appears to be thinking too much may be considered a werewolf. There may be some trouble before I, the lords, or Captain Stuart can come and explain the situation. That's why I didn't want you to change."

"But my smell is so much better when I walk as a wolf. I have to admit that it's easier to think when I'm a human, but following a trail isn't hard. Though, here it's much harder. The scent is very strong in one place, but then it just vanishes."

"Like someone put the necklace into something else?"

"Yes! Exactly!" Daniel said, excited.

"Can't you smell the person who found it?"

"Probably." Daniel nodded thoughtfully. Ethan crossed his arms and waited, hardly breathing. "However, there are too many scents in that corridor. Some are older, some are newer. Since the necklace smell is really strong, I'm not sure when it was found, and with a hundred scents around it, I have no idea by whom. Even if I smelled someone from that corridor again, I wouldn't know if that person took the necklace or not."

"Right." Ethan sighed and sat down on a chair. "Maybe we could think of some way of finding it again."

"I could go around the castle and visit the people—"

A knock stopped Daniel's reply. Both Ethan and Daniel looked at the door. "Come in!" Ethan called, curious to see who was on the other side of the door. The door opened, and Captain Stuart limped inside. Every step was accompanied by a clang of his cane. He stopped when he spotted Daniel, who watched his cane curiously. Ethan wondered if Daniel thought the cane was a toy. An image of Daniel in wolf form taking the captain's cane and running with it in his mouth flashed in front of Ethan's eyes, and the corners of his mouth twitched. He quickly pushed the image aside.

"Captain!" he said as he stood up. He motioned to Daniel. "I'm not sure if you and Daniel have met already." Daniel tore his eyes off the captain's cane and looked at Ethan.

"No, Your Majesty," Captain Stuart answered woodenly, glancing at Daniel. "I haven't had the privilege of meeting Daniel, though I noticed him upon his arrival. So did the guards and the servants, if I might add."

Ethan looked at Daniel, who was looking from him to the captain and back again. There was a confused expression on his face. Ethan looked at Captain Stuart, who looked a little uneasy. "What is it, Captain?" Ethan asked, realizing that Captain Stuart probably hadn't come to meet Daniel.

"I just received some news from Lieutenant Ernest. A witness spotted a strange man in the city this morning—very tall and dark with glowing green eyes. I didn't manage to see Rex during the time when the werewolves were staying in the castle, but I would bet anything that it's him. I am to understand that he's rather dangerous. I ordered the guards to search the city and find him. The search is already taking place, but I don't think that they will find anything."

"I see." Ethan nodded. "He's most likely after the necklace. Right now we have to hope that the necklace is still in the castle, far from his reach. We really need to find it. Daniel was just saying something to that effect when you arrived." He turned to Daniel and nodded encouragingly.

"I can try to sniff it out," Daniel said. Captain Stuart's eyes flicked to Daniel's face again. "The necklace has a specific smell, and if I were to turn to wolf, I could smell it much more easily. I would recognize that scent anywhere."

"That's great," Ethan said with a sigh. "However, if you walk around in wolf form, people will get nervous, especially after the war with Wolfast. But I think there is a way to deal with this." He turned to the captain, who eyed Daniel with suspicion. "Captain," Ethan said, and Captain Stuart looked at him. "I want you to take Daniel with you when he's in wolf form. Go through every room in the castle and check everything. When you are with others, treat Daniel like a very smart dog. Don't overdo it though."

"Don't worry, Sire," Captain Stuart said with a small bow of his head. "I completely understand what you mean. And I think that it's an excellent idea. People will feel better if they don't see Daniel as a threat. Yet, I would recommend focusing on the servants first. Searching rooms of your guests might be seen as a bit … invasive."

"I will leave the arrangements to you," Ethan said, silently agreeing with the captain. He turned to Daniel. "Are you okay with this?"

"What does it mean 'treat me like a very smart dog'?" Daniel asked with furrows on his forehead. He looked from Ethan to Captain Stuart.

"Ehm … It means that he will tell you what to do in short sentences and accompany you through the castle. If you smell something, bark in that direction and then lead the captain forward."

"Can wolves bark?" Captain Stuart asked with a momentary frown.

"Bark?" Daniel asked, looking puzzled.

"Make a sound," Ethan explained. "Give some sign to Captain Stuart, something that will let him know that you have found something." Daniel watched Ethan with a puzzled look on his face and then slowly nodded. Ethan wasn't sure if Daniel understood him properly. It felt weird. Now Daniel seemed like a slow learner, quite the opposite from the incredibly smart boy Ethan had met before the victory fight with the werewolves.

"You can go right now," Ethan said.

Captain Stuart looked at Daniel and then back at Ethan. He saluted. "Permission to prepare things, Sire?" he asked. "The servants will be very nervous if I go there with a dog right away. Also, I need to call the servants away from their rooms at the same time and keep an eye on them. For this I need the guards. If the search starts right away, I will have to go from one room to the next, giving the person who took the necklace the chance to change the hiding place without us noticing it."

"Right," Ethan said. "Daniel. Please, go to your quarters and wait there for the captain. To your room," Ethan added when he saw Daniel's blank look.

Daniel looked at Captain Stuart and then back at Ethan. It seemed as if he wanted to ask something. He stood in the middle of the room, watching Ethan for a while. Then he nodded and spun around. Barefoot, he left Ethan's quarters, his feet shuffling on the marble floor of the corridor. The captain watched Daniel until Daniel closed the door behind him. When they were left alone, he turned to Ethan. He seemed to be preoccupied with something. He opened his mouth to say something but closed it after a short hesitation.

"I will leave the arrangements to you," Ethan said. Captain Stuart saluted and spun around. He left the room, leaving Ethan alone with his thoughts. Ethan looked at the piece of cloth on the floor. He walked to the cloth and picked it up, throwing it towards the table that held the bowl.

There was a strange feeling building up in him. Daniel was going through a strange phase, but Ethan couldn't figure out what exactly it was. He had bigger troubles to figure out at the moment. If Rex got the necklace, they all would be in serious trouble.

CHAPTER 4

B ess must have read a hundred documents in the library of the fortress, but he still hadn't found any relevant information; at least not relevant to him. He was about to give up, believing that he had hit a dead end, when he noticed a very slim book on the shelf, nearly completely hidden between two huge volumes on the history of Wolfast.

It was difficult to get the book off the shelf because the books were stuck together. It took Bess nearly a minute, but in the end, he held a slim book with a white cover in his hands. He opened it and read the first page: "How Magic Works in Lanland and Tasks of The League".

Bess frowned and turned the page. The book contained only thirty pages, which described magic. There were various sections of information on energy and matter, including the conversion of energy when a werewolf changes. He kept on reading, not sure how true the information was.

According to the book, werewolves were actually mortal. The bite started a chain reaction in the body of a werewolf. It was a disease, though ironically, this disease prolonged the individual's life. As Bess read on, he found out that he wasn't going to live forever. The disease would kill him in a few millennia. That wasn't so bad. However, the disease also hurt a werewolf's brain. That explained some behaviour of the werewolves. Bess wondered how long it would take for him to become the monster like the other werewolves in Wolfast.

He turned the page, hoping to find a cure, or at least a way how to slow the process down. The next page dealt with lightning, but the description was too complicated for Bess to understand. He returned to the previous page, trying to find more information on werewolves, but the author of the book hadn't bothered with any.

He sighed and continued reading the book. He half expected to find some information on Rex in there. There had to be something relevant about him. Rex didn't look like an ordinary guy. There was no description of anything that remotely reminded Bess of Rex. Feeling a little disappointed, he reached the last page. A pamphlet fell onto the table. He picked it up, putting the book aside. The pamphlet was small, only a few pages. It was handwritten and looked as if it used to be part of something bigger.

Curious, he started to read it. As his eyes moved through the page, he turned paler and paler until he was completely white. He finished reading and slammed the pamphlet against the table, his hands shaking. It wasn't so much the information the pamphlet contained that made him nervous; it was the fact most things were coming true, and if the rest became reality …

He jumped to his feet and started to pace back and forth in the small space. He ran his fingers through his hair and dug deep into his scalp. The ribbon that was keeping his hair in a neat hairstyle became untied and fell to the ground. Bess ignored it.

He had to get to Norene right away. He had to inform Ethan about the threat. He wasn't even worried about breaking the truce. If Rex got to the necklace, there wouldn't be any Norene or Wolfast, so the truce wouldn't matter anymore. The only thing that mattered was getting the information to Ethan right away.

He grabbed the pamphlet and stuck it into his pocket. He whirled around and bolted out of the library, still shaking. He ran through the corridors and out into the yard, nearly crashing to a few guards on his way. He stopped in the middle of the yard and looked around, his untied hair getting into his eyes. He pushed the hair aside and hurried through the yard towards the gate.

Some guards saluted him, but he ignored them. He stopped by the tall main gate and, with one hand, opened the right door. The guard who stood by the guard house was about to say something, but as soon as the gate moved, he dropped the tin cup he'd been holding to the ground. He watched Bess, his mouth gaping. As Bess stepped through the gate, his gaze fell on a mechanism for opening the gate. The mechanism seemed to be operated by at least two people. That, at least, explained the shock on the guard's face.

He spun around and closed the gate after him, flashing the stunned guard a bright smile.

Lord Adrian walked towards the library with a book in his hand. It was King Peter's diary. He had decided to go through all the diaries and put together the history of Norene through the kings' points of view. It would be interesting reading. Though there were many books on history of Norene, each showed the history in a slightly different light. Lord Adrian believed that the information in the diaries was the closest to the real history since the diary entries were written right after specific events. Of course, these were subjective depictions of the events, but so were all of them, even the ones by the historians.

Only King John I hadn't known that his diary would be read in the future. The other diaries had already been filtered and edited by the kings who wrote them. No one wanted to look bad, so they tried to write the information down in the best possible light, not always succeeding. Lord Adrian only wished someone would have started this tradition before King John I. There was always a lord responsible for Norene, so there was always someone who was in the middle of the events, but only King John I actually wrote his thoughts down. Though there were only a few diaries, these were very interesting reading.

He entered the library and walked over to the shelf where the diaries were kept. He wanted to return the diary, but there were no diaries on the shelf. He stopped and looked around. The diaries were scattered on the table by the window. He walked over to them and, one by one, returned them to the shelf. Once he was finished, he found out that the first diary of King John I and the last one of Ethan's father were missing. Lord Adrian knew that Ethan kept his diary with him at all times. Maybe, he had taken his father's diary too.

There had been a librarian in the past, but since the death of the last one three years ago, no one had taken over the job. No one wanted it because people believed it was cursed. What a superstition—just because the last one was crushed by a fallen statue, the one before that drowned in a puddle of rain water, and the one before that stubbed his toe and fell in front of a running horse. Maybe it was once again time to search for a librarian. It needn't be someone tough; just someone who could keep the library in order and look after the books. And someone who wouldn't die of a weird death.

Lady Joan entered the library and stopped. She held King John I's diary in her hands. Lord Adrian looked at the book in her hands and then smiled at her. "I see you're also reading the diaries," he said.

"Oh, I just started," she said, walking up to the shelf. "I see that someone tidied them up," she added as she returned the dairy to the shelf. "Was it you?" she asked. Lord Adrian nodded. "If you hadn't done it, I would have."

"Did you pull them all out?"

"No, I think Captain Stuart did. I believe he was looking for King Philip's diary. I assume. He looked very angry as he was shuffling through the diaries on the table, but he didn't take anything. You know Captain Stuart; he never answers any of my questions. Maybe he answers yours," she added with a smile as she pulled out the next diary.

"I think he answers only the king's questions," Lord Adrian said pensively while Lady Joan leafed through the booklet. "At least I never tried asking him something. How did you like the diary?"

"It was incredible!" Lady Joan exclaimed. She looked at Lord Adrian with excitement on her face. "I hardly breathed when I read about the battle. I would be so scared if I had to stand up to a werewolf! I always knew that King John was a hero and a remarkable man, but only now do I feel as if I truly know him. Before, he was our first king in a thousand years, and the man who freed us, but now I see him also as a father and a husband who wanted a better country for his children and grandchildren and for people of Norene. I think that his motives were wonderful. I can see how he managed to make people fight for their freedom. This was never about him; this was about their future."

"Nicely put," Lord Adrian said with a smile.

He understood why Ethan fancied her. She was smart and passionate. She treated people with respect, yet she wasn't scared. She most likely spoke to Ethan as if he were a normal man. Ethan had never been much for ceremony. His father was often angry about that, but because of it, Ethan felt more like the people's king than any king before him.

"I just wonder why there are so many diaries," Lady Joan said suddenly. "Or more precisely, so many kings," she corrected herself.

"King John was quite old, so the beginning saw a lot of changes in a short time. Ethan is actually the first young king … well, the second. But King Thomas ruled for only a few weeks. Nevertheless, Ethan is the youngest king of Norene."

"I believe he's very lucky," Lady Joan said suddenly.

"Why is that?"

"He's surrounded now with wonderful people," Lady Joan said with a smile. "I actually thought that you would be a little angry at how the things turned out."

"Why would that be?" Lord Adrian asked surprised.

"If King Philip died two months earlier, you would have been the king. Most people in that situation would feel resentment."

"Maybe," Lord Adrian said. He could feel he was flushing. "I actually thought a lot about that," he admitted. He looked at all the diaries on the shelf and shrugged. "The truth is that I was getting nervous when King Philip got ill. I was already of age, but Ethan wasn't. It wouldn't have felt right. Some say I would be king, but there is a law that would make me only a temporary king, since Ethan was already over fifteen. And seeing Ethan's difficult start, I'm actually glad I didn't have to deal with that. This way I have a lot of privileges but not so many responsibilities. I look after the castle and advise the king. No, I wouldn't have traded with him."

"As I said," Lady Joan said with a smile, "the king is lucky to have such a great person for a friend."

Lord Adrian wasn't sure what to say. He decided to change the subject completely. "There's a masquerade planned. I'm sure that His Majesty would be thrilled if you joined us. It will be here in the castle."

"I would love to come," Lady Joan said politely.

Lady Joan's matter-of-fact tone of voice made Lord Adrian hesitate for a moment. "The king has already invited you, hasn't he?" he asked with a smile.

Lady Joan blushed and looked down. "Yes, he has," she answered. A radiant smile appeared on her face.

"I will inform you of the time and place once it's settled," Lord Adrian said, and he walked towards the library door. He stopped at the threshold and turned to Lady Joan. "I recommend King Thomas's diary. It's very short, but the tenth entry is rather amusing."

"Wasn't he the one who thought that he could actually fly?" Lady Joan asked, surprised.

"Yes." Lord Adrian nodded with a smile and left.

Christine stirred in her dream, murmuring under her breath. The bed was so warm and cosy. She could have stayed in the soft bedding for ages. A knock reached her ears. She stirred some more and then, with the force of her will, opened her eyes. It was very bright outside. She had obviously overslept.

The knocking continued. It was still fairly polite knocking, so she took her time as she climbed out of the bed. She was in no mood to meet anyone. She hoped that whoever was at the door would give up and leave. She rubbed her eyes and looked around for her dressing gown. It was on the chair in the corner. She stood up and picked up the dressing gown as the knock sounded again. She put it on and, feeling a little lightheaded and confused, she staggered to the door. She was incredibly thirsty. She tied the belt of the gown and opened the door a fraction. John stood on the other side. He looked relieved when he saw her. "What are you doing here?" she asked, surprised, as she opened the door wide to let him in.

"I came to say goodbye," he said calmly, remaining in the corridor. "I didn't have a chance in the office, so I came here."

"What are you talking about?"

"I'm leaving the city," John said, avoiding Christine's stare. Christine's jaw dropped. "I've decided that this life is way too thrilling and dangerous," John continued, glancing at Christine. "I miss the calmness of the fields. The only work with wood I had was for that one picture. I'm not that keen on running after murderers through the city. The city is very noisy and dangerous for my taste."

"When are you leaving?" Christine asked. She felt a strange pressure on her chest. She had just realized that she would actually miss him.

"In an hour. I spoke to Edmund, and he agrees that he has no use for me here. He thought there would be more pictures. We have an agreement.

If there are any images needed for a book in the future, he will send me a picture, and I will carve it and send it back. However, there are no pictures planned for the next four books that are to be published. I believe two are philosophical and one is mathematical, so there is no requirement for illustrations."

"What time is it?" Christine asked, confused. She thought it was morning.

"It's four in the afternoon … maybe later. It was four when I left the office. Edmund was a little nervous when you didn't come in. I promised I would check up on you and let him know before I left the city. He wanted to get me a carriage, but the mail coach is good enough for me. It leaves in an hour, so I'd better hurry."

"Good luck," Christine said meekly. They stood still for a while, looking at each other. Christine wasn't sure if she should say something to persuade John to stay. She wondered if she wanted John to stay because he was useful to The Royal Press, or because she had got used to him. There was also a third option, which she wasn't ready to admit yet.

John smiled feebly and turned his back to Christine. Slowly, he walked down the corridor, not looking back at her. Christine watched after him until he vanished down the stairs. She expected him to look up at her from the stairs, but he avoided her gaze.

Slowly, she closed the door and leaned against it. Some part of her hoped that she would now wake up and find out that all this was a dream, but she knew it wasn't. She had no reason to feel sad about John's leaving. She hardly knew the guy. Yet tears reached her cheeks and continued to her chin. She wiped her right cheek. The drop on her left cheek fell off her chin to the ground. She sighed and buried her face in her hands. She felt tired. She just wanted to sit down and cry.

She straightened up and lifted her head up high. She would not cry for anyone. There was no point in that. John was leaving, and she didn't need him. She was planning on looking for the Masked Man on her own anyway. John was too afraid for their safety.

She wiped her eyes and walked to the window. Out there somewhere, the Masked Man was hiding. She had to find him; she had to warn him. She looked at the rooftops, hoping to glimpse anything useful. Then her gaze fell onto the street. Near the corner, she spotted John walking up the street. His head was low, and his hands were in his pockets. He looked sad, hunched down like that. Her heart hurt at the sight of him, walking away. Her eyes filled with tears again, and the pressure in her chest tightened. She spun away from the window, collapsed onto the sofa, and wept into the cushion until she ran out of tears.

A dark-black coach rattled towards Norene. Finn was sitting up on the seat, steering horses. Bess sat inside by the window watching the passing countryside. He knew he was running out of time, but he didn't want to reach Norene as a werewolf. He needed to come as a friend, which was difficult when he was in wolf form.

The hills of the north were already visible on the horizon. Bess knew that the border with Norene was approaching. He'd had the long drive to come up with a plan, but nothing had come to his mind. He had no business entering Norene, especially in his position as ruler of Wolfast. According to the agreement, he was risking another war with Ethan. He could only hope that Ethan would rather hear him out than start an open war right away. Ethan wasn't a crazy werewolf.

Even though Bess was the ruler of Wolfast—or maybe for exactly that reason—he knew he would have trouble getting into Norenc. Werewolves weren't really welcomed in Norene at the moment. He needed some way of persuading the guards to let him through. Telling them who he was would not be an option. He needed something else—a good background story.

Then a thought came to his mind. He rummaged through the contents of his bag and produced a blank parchment. He pulled out a quill and ink and wrote a short letter. Luckily, he had seen many letters like this one, so he knew what to write.

Bess peeked outside and saw three guards on the road. They waited for the coach to approach. His heart racing, he quickly finished the letter and put the quill and ink away. He folded the parchment just as Finn called from the top of the coach. "Bess, they're asking me to stop. Do I stop?"

"Yes," Bess called back. He didn't want to cause trouble, especially since there was a fragile truce between the countries. If he caused trouble on the borders, he could have trouble reaching the king.

The coach stopped, and one of the guards walked over to the coach's door. Bess was sitting on the cushion, leaning towards the window, trying to look as normal as possible.

"Good afternoon, sir," the guard said with a smile. There was something strange in his expression. The smile looked friendly, but the sword in his right hand definitely didn't. "What is your business in Norene?"

"I'm from Thornari," Bess lied calmly. "There are some barrels for my wine ready for me in Norene." He laughed merrily but stopped abruptly when the guard narrowed his eyes.

"It's a long drive from Thornari all the way through Wolfast just for barrels," the guard said suspiciously, the smile completely vanishing from his face. "And your coach doesn't look like it could carry any barrels."

"I'm not carrying the barrels in this coach," Bess said with a merry laughter, and he waived his hand dismissively. "That would be silly. No, there is already a cart in Eblestone. But it's not very comfortable for a long drive. I wouldn't travel all the way here just to inspect the barrels, but my wife insisted. These are special barrels, and she wanted to be sure that they are well built. This is merely a formality; your carpenters in Eblestone are the best in Lanland, after all," he added with a bright smile. He could feel sweat erupt on his forehead. Why had he chosen this story? He felt as if it was the stupidest thing to say.

Bess could see the guard's chest rose with pride. The carpenters in Eblestone were indeed well known wide and far. "Do you have a receipt or document confirming this story?" the guard asked in much nicer tone.

Bess quickly produced the letter he had just written. He had tried to make it look as official as he could. Since he didn't have paper, which had been used in Norene for decades now, he had made it a two-way letter. One page contained a letter from Francois—a name that sounded like it belonged to someone from Thornari—requesting barrels; the second page contained a response from a carpenter, John Johnson, that the barrels were ready, and Francois could come for them after the seventh day of the following month. Bess counted on John being name so often used in families that a carpenter with that name actually existed.

The guard read the letter and frowned. "I don't think there is any John Johnson in Eblestone," he said.

"I hope you're wrong," Bess said with a fake laugh. His skin crawled. "I have already sent an advance payment for the barrels."

The guard looked up at Bess and then at the other guards. "Do you know any John Johnson in Eblestone?" he called at other guards.

Bess couldn't see the other guard, but he heard an answer: "I think it's John Ericson's son. He's also a carpenter."

"All right then," the guard said, and he handed Bess the letter. Bess suppressed an urge to breathe out with relief. "Have a good day," the guard said, and he waved at Finn, who snapped the reins. The coach rattled forward with a relieved Bess in the seat.

They drove for a while, and then Finn called from his seat: "That was neat."

Bess grinned and nodded, feeling proud of himself. Then his smile froze. He leaned out of the window, glancing at the road behind them. The boarder was far behind them. "Yes," he said to Finn, "but I have to come up with something better for the castle guards."

CHAPTER 5

Captain Stuart knocked on Lord Charles's door and waited, leaning against his cane. He wasn't so keen on taking a wolf on a tour of the castle, but he had to admit that it was a good idea. For weeks he'd had no idea why the werewolves wanted Daniel. The necklace explained a lot, though he didn't understand the importance of the necklace. It was brand-new information, and he wasn't going to question the king on this one. If the king was right and the necklace was dangerous, they had to find it. If Rex was in the city, they didn't have much time.

Mary opened the door. She froze for a moment when she spotted Captain Stuart, but then she stepped aside to let him enter. He bit his tongue and didn't point out that they were lords now and had servants to open the door. He just nodded instead of a greeting and entered.

"Where is Daniel?" he asked as the door closed behind him.

"Here," a voice said from the other side of the room. Captain Stuart turned around to see Daniel by the window. He had a keen expression on his face.

"We'd better get ready," Captain Stuart said calmly. "The servants are all in the main hall, and a few guards are keeping an eye on them. The servants aren't very nervous at the moment, but they might get restless if we're too long. We have about an hour to walk through their rooms. I don't want to detain them very long. They have work to do."

"Okay," Daniel said with a shrug, and he stepped towards the door.

"You should change here," Captain Stuart said as he stepped into Daniel's path. "We don't want anyone to see you change. It's safer this way."

Daniel looked at Mary and then back at Captain Stuart. Captain Stuart didn't move. He knew that the servants would leave very quickly if they thought that Daniel was a real werewolf. Daniel stood still for a moment and then shrugged and pulled off his shirt.

"I was also thinking of calling you Canissi while you're a wolf," Captain Stuart added as Daniel pulled down his trousers. Mary turned bright red and quickly turned away. She blabbed something Captain Stuart didn't catch and then dashed out.

"What's wrong with 'Daniel'?" Daniel asked, surprised. He pulled the trousers off his feet, threw them into the corner, and straightened up in front of Captain Stuart.

"It's a nice name," Captain Stuart said, unmoved by Daniel's stripping. "However, I don't want to make a connection between the wolf that will walk with me and you. It's for your safety."

"Why?"

"No particular reason," Captain Stuart said, trying to sound sincere. He didn't want to go to too much detail on the mentality of the servants and the guards. "It's just a precaution," he added with a forced smile.

"What's a precaution?"

Captain Stuart hesitated. He thought that Daniel was supposed to be at least as smart as a werewolf, but then he remembered the werewolves who had resided in the castle during the war. Compared to most of them, Daniel was a genius. "It means to take action to avoid a bad thing in the future."

"What bad thing?"

"We don't have time for this," Captain Stuart said impatiently. "Please, change and let's go."

Daniel opened his mouth as if he wanted to object, but then he just shrugged. Suddenly, his body started to change. For Captain Stuart this was a vision that would haunt his dreams for a long time.

Daniel's body deformed in a series of moves. First his eyes turned orange. Then they took on a very unhuman form. There was a moment when Daniel looked like a human yet didn't look like a human at all. The hair on Captain Stuart's arms and neck stood up. He took a step back, unable to tear his eyes off Daniel. Daniel's nose started to move forward, his chin moved higher, his eyes changed shape, and his ears moved to the top of his head, changing shape as they moved. The hair on his head and body got lighter and longer as it turned to fur. His skin started to wriggle as if something was trying to get out of his body. More hair erupted all over his body as it also underwent dramatic changes. His hands and legs were getting smaller, and his back became hunched. A tail appeared from nowhere and grew bigger. At one point, the creature in front of the captain wasn't human, yet still wasn't a wolf. It was some hideous hybrid, uglier than a werewolf in wolf form.

Captain Stuart closed his eyes, trying to suppress the image of the change. He took a deep breath and reopened his eyes just in time to see a wolf with nearly completely white fur walk by. The captain gulped and turned towards the door. Daniel stood in front of the door, watching him. Captain Stuart shook vigorously and swallowed. The transformation was obviously over, and now a fully-grown wolf with a curious look on his face stood by the door.

"All right," Captain Stuart said and walked towards Daniel, leaning on his cane. "Let's do this, Canissi." Daniel tilted his head to one side. "It actually means puppy in an ancient language," Captain Stuart said as he opened the door. They both stepped onto the corridor. He had no idea why he had said that. He just felt better, at the moment, when he was talking. It helped him to keep his mind off the change. "I know that you're not a puppy, but it's a nice name. I once had a dog who had that name. He was very smart, though not as smart as you. And he was also smaller."

Daniel put his snout to the floor and sniffed it as he walked after Captain Stuart. Captain Stuart led the way to the lower floors of the castle where the servants lived.

"If you smell anything, make a noise," Captain Stuart continued. "And try not to do too many things on your own. If I say something, do it right away. We need to give the impression that you're a dog. And dogs are trained to listen to humans."

Daniel whined behind Captain Stuart. Captain Stuart turned around and stopped. Daniel stood in the middle of the corridor, his head tilted to left. He watched Captain Stuart with a dog-like expression. For a moment Captain Stuart felt as if he was talking to a real dog.

"What's unclear?" he asked nervously. Daniel still watched him without moving a muscle. Captain Stuart felt a little annoyed at the moment. "Look," he said and lowered his voice. "We need to do this quickly. Please don't linger."

Daniel decided to let slip whatever had surprised him, and he walked around Captain Stuart. He hurried down the corridor so fast that Captain Stuart had a hard time keeping up. They walked through the castle until they reached the corridor where the servants lived. The captain walked down the corridor, reaching for his keys. The corridor was filled with guards who didn't look at all surprised to see Captain Stuart with a wolf by his side. Captain Stuart didn't pay the guards any attention. He walked to the first door, the sound of his cane being the only sound in the corridor. He produced the keys, opened the door, and let Daniel enter first. Then he followed him, absentmindedly closing the door after him.

Daniel walked around the room, sniffing everything. He poked at the sheets of the bed, fell flat onto his stomach to check beneath the bed, and he even sniffed inside the slippers. Then he stopped by the wardrobe, stood on his hind legs, and pulled the doorknob of the wardrobe with his paw. He jumped down, opened the door ajar with his snout, and stuck his head inside.

Captain Stuart walked over to him just in case someone entered. Daniel was sniffing each article of clothing, one by one. Then he spun around and walked to the front door. Captain Stuart grabbed the wardrobe door calmly, ready to close it. Out of the corner of his eye he saw that Daniel had opened the front door with his paw.

Captain Stuart became nervous. He worried that Daniel would try to open the next door too, which might be suspicious to the guards. He slammed the wardrobe closed and hurried after Daniel. When he marched into the corridor, he stopped. Daniel stood in front of the next door, looking at it calmly. The guards looked a little bored as they watched them. Captain Stuart wasn't sure if Daniel had tried to open the door or not, but it seemed that he was waiting for him. Daniel was obviously smarter than an average werewolf.

Captain Stuart unlocked the door, trying to look as if that had been part of the plan, and let Daniel inside. Daniel immediately rushed into the room and checked it just as quickly as he had checked the first one. Captain Stuart was glad Daniel didn't linger. He was a bit nervous about the whole situation and didn't want to spend too much time in the rooms. Daniel checked the bed, the wardrobe, the nightstand, and every item in the room. It took him less than a minute.

Like this, without any change, they walked from room to room until they reached the end of the corridor. Captain Stuart followed Daniel, getting bored. The search was tedious since every room looked basically the same. Daniel's excitement from the first room lasted him till the middle of the corridor. From there, he continued the search with less and less energy. The necklace was nowhere to be found. Captain Stuart wasn't surprised.

Suddenly, with two more rooms to go, Daniel stopped and sniffed the air. Captain Stuart stopped, excitement pouring into his body. Daniel turned around, still sniffing the air. There was some murmuring between the guards. Daniel moved to the nearest guard and sniffed his trousers. Captain Stuart felt disappointment. There was no way that the guard had the necklace. Not that the captain had any illusions about his men; he just knew that no one would be that stupid. Even if the guard had found the necklace, he wouldn't have taken it to the search. It would now be locked up somewhere in the barracks. There had to be something else in his pockets; something that took Daniel's focus off the task at hand.

"What do you have in your trouser pockets?" Captain Stuart barked. The guard nervously reached inside and produced a piece of cloth. He unwrapped it and revealed a little remnant of a sandwich. Daniel snatched it from the guard and gulped it down without even chewing it.

"Canissi!" Captain Stuart snapped at Daniel, who ignored him. Daniel turned his back to the stunned guard, who still looked at the cloth in disbelief. Daniel stopped in front of another door. He looked at Captain Stuart and then at the door handle. Then he looked at the crack between the door and the frame, sniffing at the door. Captain Stuart watched Daniel, who didn't pay him any attention. The captain stood still for a few seconds. Then he sighed and unlocked the door. The sooner this was over, the better.

However, nothing was revealed in either of the last two rooms. Captain Stuart sent the guards away and then walked Daniel back to his quarters, thinking hard. Did it mean that the necklace had never been there, or that it was concealed? The more Captain Stuart thought about the possibilities, the scarier the whole situation seemed. The necklace could be anywhere. It could be on its way to Rex at that very moment.

Captain Stuart opened the door for Daniel, and they both entered the anteroom of Lord Charles's chambers. Daniel started to change right away.

This time Captain Stuart turned his back to the spectacle. He patiently waited for Daniel to speak.

"I hoped we would find it," Daniel said behind Captain Stuart. Captain Stuart turned back and was relieved to see Daniel in human form. He didn't mind that Daniel was nude as long as he looked like a human or like a wolf. The stage in between was revolting. Daniel walked to the window and picked up his trousers. "It should have worked," Daniel added as he pulled the trousers on.

"Were there no traces of it anywhere?" Captain Stuart asked. Daniel shook his head and put on the shirt. He turned around, tucking the shirt into the trousers. Captain Stuart felt disappointed. He hadn't expected to find the necklace, yet part of him had really hoped that they would. "It was either in a container the whole time, or it wasn't there at all. I would think the second one is correct. Whoever took the necklace would probably hide it elsewhere. No one wants to be connected with the theft, though I wouldn't call finding a necklace in a corridor a theft. They probably sneaked out with it the next day."

"I don't know," Daniel said slowly. "Wouldn't the person who found the necklace want to check it? And where better to do this than in that small room where you live? Just opening the box and looking inside."

"Yes, I understand what you want to say, but why hide it in the room?"

"Not hiding it, just seeing it," Daniel said. Captain Stuart frowned. "The necklace has a very strong and distinct smell," Daniel explained. "I would recognize it anywhere. It's in Ethan's room and in the library. It's very weak, fading, but I can tell that the necklace was there a long time ago. Even if the box had been open for only a short time, I would be able to smell it."

There were many things that Captain Stuart found wrong with that statement. First, it was weird to hear Daniel call the king by his first name. Second, the reasoning was so logical that it didn't fit Daniel at all. The wolf who had no idea what the word *precaution* meant had put together a very strong argument. And third, it was weird to hear an animal to know so much about human nature.

"The day before yesterday, I asked the servants personally if they had found the necklace," Captain Stuart said. "Before, it would be just finding it, but if they didn't say anything two days ago, it became something more serious."

"That still wouldn't change the fact one of them would open the container to have a look," Daniel pointed out.

"All right," Captain Stuart said cautiously. "It's very likely that whoever found the necklace, would check it out in his or her room. That is, however, true only if the finder took the necklace to the room rather than taking it outside the castle right away."

Daniel thought about this for a moment and then shrugged. "Could be, but I still feel the necklace calling to me. It feels like it's still in the castle."

"Where did the trail lead you when you found it in the corridor?"

"Nowhere. It just vanished a few steps later. Whoever found it picked it up and placed it into some … container right away. On the one side the trail leads directly from Ethan's room. Then it gets very strong in the corridor, and then it vanishes."

"Someone could have taken it from the king's room," Captain Stuart pointed out.

Daniel shrugged. "I thought about that," he admitted. "When I was in Ethan's room, I smelled quite a few people. Five scents stood out: Ethan's, yours, Lord James's, Lord Adrian's, and a servant's—the one who gets very annoyed when you sniff his hands." Captain Stuart closed his eyes after this statement. He decided to let it slide. "Lord James, Lord Adrian, and you do not smell like the necklace, so I don't think that you found it," Daniel continued calmly. "The smell in that corridor is much more intense than anywhere else—except Ethan's room and office—so it seems that the necklace was there for a long time."

Captain Stuart blinked. This had to be what it would feel like to have a conversation with a dog who could talk. They obviously saw the world differently. The smells were very strong. These were additional clues to the mystery. "If I understand you correctly, the conclusion is that whoever found the necklace put it into a pocket, or—"

"Not a normal pocket," Daniel interrupted him. "It had to be something that would hide the scent of the necklace."

"A leather bag? Like a money pouch?"

"I have no idea what that is," Daniel said calmly.

"So, the king lost the necklace in the corridor. Then someone else came along a little while later and picked it up. He or she put it into something and walked away. Probably not a servant, but someone else? Maybe a guard?"

"Yes! We could go and check the barracks!"

"Maybe we should, but not now," Captain Stuart said, and he turned to the door. He took two steps, leaning against his cane. Then he stopped and turned back. "Wait a minute! You can smell if someone held the necklace?"

"Yes," Daniel said with a short nod. "If the person held the necklace for a few minutes, the scent would last for a few days."

"What if the person washes his or her hands?"

"The scent is very strong. It overpowers other smells. I can still smell the necklace on Ethan. I can smell better in wolf form, so I would even smell small traces that are leaking from some sort of box, for example. But I believe I could smell the necklace if someone held it."

"Maybe we shouldn't go around checking rooms and places. Maybe we should check the people." Captain Stuart thought about this for a while and then smiled a nasty smile. "Change back and come with me."

Christine entered the main office of The Royal Press. She couldn't just sit at home. Maybe she hoped that she would meet John on her way, or crash into him in the office. She knew that was unlikely since the coach had left over an hour ago, but she still hoped for something, though she wasn't sure what it was.

It was after six o'clock in the evening, so Christine hadn't expected anyone to be in, but everyone save John was still at work. As she closed the door behind her, the murmur inside ceased. It felt like a slap to Christine. She jumped with fright and leaned against the door. She looked around, startled, looking from one curious face to another. She stood there in awkward silence, not sure what to say.

The door of Edmund's office flew open, and Edmund stepped outside, holding a piece of paper in his hand. There were huge letters in the centre. Obviously, they were still sorting out the title of the book they were publishing.

Edmund froze and looked around surprised. "What's wrong?" he asked the guys and then looked at the entrance door. "There you are!" he said as soon as he spotted Christine. "We've all been worried sick about you!" He stepped back towards his office and motioned for Christine to follow him. Christine walked over there feeling the stares of her colleagues on her. She wanted to turn around and run away, but when she entered the privacy of the office, she felt relief. Edmund closed the door behind her and walked over to his table.

Christine sagged into the chair on the other side of the table, noticing that her hands were shaking slightly. "What's going on?" she asked.

"We were concerned about you," Edmund explained. "We all were, but most of all John."

"He's always nervous, so maybe this time it had nothing to do with me," Christine pointed out. She clutched the armrests of the chair without noticing it.

"Who can blame him?" Edmund asked. "We haven't had this many murders since that maniac was hunting down and murdering the fat guys—whatever happened to him." He put down the paper he still held. Christine spotted that they had tried to split the title of the book onto three lines. The paper read

The brief history of the former ruler of Norene Wolfast
from a werewolf's perspective, or how we became such enemies.
War diaries of Norene and Wolfast.

Edmund sat down opposite Christine. Christine looked away to avoid his stare. She fixed her gaze on a little leaf that was on the floor beneath the table. Edmund leaned against the table between them.

"John wasn't useful anyway," Christine said, still avoiding Edmund's stare. "It's not like we're going to miss him."

"Not really," Edmund said, eyeing Christine. She looked up. "I felt safer knowing that you weren't running after the Masked Man alone. John could find you anywhere. I don't think anyone else ever got to you so quickly." These words stung Christine in the chest like a dagger. She opened her mouth to retort, but Edmund continued calmly: "And it was interesting to have a drawing of the ball. There are some artists in the city who would be willing to draw something interesting, but there aren't many carpenters who could put it into wooden form. Too bad we won't be using that in the future."

"I thought you had an agreement with him," Christine said confused. "He mentioned that if you needed an illustration, you would send him an image for carving."

"Really?" Edmund said, surprised. "Maybe he mentioned that as a possibility, yet we didn't agree on anything. I like the idea, though. Maybe I will try it out. Though I should write to him and check with him and make sure he's okay with that sort of arrangement. Or maybe not. I don't have any images planned, and people aren't expecting any. Maybe I should leave the drawings in the books and keep *The Royal Messenger* the same for now. We need to sort out the technology. Even with wooden carvings of the drawings, we can't print too many copies. That's why we switched to metal letters. It lasts longer, you know. The drawings would have to be in soft wood so that the carpenter could carve it in detail, and soft wood wouldn't last long enough."

"Sure," Christine said curly. "Anything else?"

"What? Oh … yes, just one small thing," Edmund said as he picked up a quill. "Take a day off," he said without looking at Christine. "Or better yet, two. You look like you need some sleep." Edmund pulled the paper with the book's title closer and underlined the last sentence of the title.

"I'm all right," Christine snapped.

Edmund looked up from the paper and pierced Christine with his stare. "You don't look it," he said calmly. "There is no news right now, and if something comes up, the guys can deal with it. It's only two days. I'm sure you can survive two days of leisure."

"I can also survive two days of work," Christine added.

"I know," Edmund said with a short nod. "But right now, you need sleep more than I need you here."

"What if something happens? What if you need to renew *The Freedom Speaker*? I wrote most of those articles!" Christine knew that it was feeble reason, and Edmund's understanding smile made her blush.

"It's only two days," he said calmly. "If something happens, I know where to find you. Otherwise, see you next week," he added as he wrote a note on the paper. Christine had no idea what he had written. She had given up trying to read Edmund's incredibly untidy handwriting a long time ago—especially upside down.

She stood up, her brain racing in search of possible arguments against days off. Nothing came to her mind. Edmund kept on writing, occasionally glancing at Christine. She knew there was no point in playing who-will-break-the-awkward-silence-first game because Edmund was excellent at that one.

She spun around and marched out of Edmund's office. She hurried through the room, being watched the whole time by her colleagues. She stopped only when she reached the street. She had no idea what to do next. She felt like crying. Her head was hurting, and so she decided to go home. What was the point anyway? She was completely and utterly useless. She might as well stop trying.

CHAPTER 6

It was late evening, and Ethan sat in his office. He was leaning his head against his hands, elbows on the table, looking at the wall opposite. He was tempted to ask Lady Joan to ride with him in the forests. He imagined the whole event. A smile appeared on his face as he imagined the scene. Suddenly, the door opened, and Daniel stepped inside, looking slightly disappointed.

Ethan sighed and straightened up. "It didn't go as planned?" he asked Daniel. Daniel sagged into the chair and shook his head. He rubbed his eyes and yawned. "Not even a trace?" Ethan asked, hoping against hope.

"No." Daniel shook his head again. "I smell it now very faintly, because you used to wear it, but other than that … it's as if the necklace vanished into thin air."

"You tried, and that's what counts," Ethan said. He leaned back. "I was really hoping you would find it, but if you can't find it, maybe Rex won't find it either. I have no idea what would happen, but every cell of my body screams that he mustn't get the necklace."

"What if he already has it?" Daniel asked curiously.

Ethan thought about this possibility. Chills ran down his spine. Out of the corner of his eye he saw that Lord Adrian was approaching the office door, which Daniel had left open. "Let's hope that's not the case," Ethan said. "Now, on a more cheerful note, have you thought what mask you will wear for the masquerade?" There was a blank expression on Daniel's face. A soft knock filled the silence, and Lord Adrian entered the office. Ethan looked at him and then turned back to Daniel.

Daniel didn't look at Lord Adrian. He just sat in the chair, watching Ethan. "What's a mask?" he asked after a while.

Ethan sighed. Explaining the easiest things in life could be so exhausting. "A mask is a thing you put on your face to look like someone or something else."

"Why?"

"You ask difficult questions," Ethan said with a smile. "Why? It's for fun. It's just make believe. You come as you, but not entirely you."

"So I can come in as a wolf?" Daniel asked, looking excited for a moment. Lord Adrian's eyes went round, and Ethan himself could imagine the situation in the ballroom. The people would definitely freak out if a real wolf came into the ballroom. And if Daniel changed in the ballroom, people would be frantic.

"The point is to go as something other than who you really are," he said patiently. "For example, I'm going as a panther. I have a mask my father used to wear, and I will wear black clothes."

"But you're not a panther," Daniel said, bewilderment rising in his voice. "You're a human."

"I know that," Ethan said wearily. Lord Adrian covered his mouth, but Ethan could clearly see he was grinning. "Maybe you could talk about this to Lord Charles. Together you can choose a mask for you. We have a few in the castle. Just don't come in wolf form, okay?"

"Okay," Daniel said slowly, looking confused. He stood up, smiled at Lord Adrian, and left the office.

Lord Adrian watched after him for a while, and then he turned to Ethan, who met his stare. "Is it me, or is Daniel much … slower in understanding things than he used to be?"

"I noticed that too," Ethan admitted. "Before it was like talking to a strange human being. He was way too smart for a wolf. He was way too smart for most humans, come to that. Now I feel as if I'm talking to a dog. Maybe we spoke with him about easier concepts before. Masquerade is somewhat weird when you come to think of it."

"True, but even Lord Charles said that he feels as if Daniel has stopped evolving. He wasn't able to understand the concept of kissing, and he kept on asking until Lord Charles gave up and asked him to stop asking. Maybe that blow in the store house caused more damage than we thought."

"I actually think that the necklace has something to do with it," Ethan said, watching after Daniel. "He gave it to me soon after he woke up from that blow. I think that the necklace was communicating with him and explaining some things to him."

"How would that even work?" Lord Adrian asked with a chuckle.

Ethan thought about this. There was something strange about the necklace. He couldn't put it out of his mind ever since he had lost it. It felt as if he had lost a friend, not a thing. The necklace was alive … in a sense. "This may sound crazy, but that necklace is no ordinary necklace," he said at last.

"I figured that out," Lord Adrian said gravely, watching Ethan intently. Ethan didn't like that look. It felt like something was wrong with him. "By the way, did they find it?" Lord Adrian asked and motioned in Daniel's direction. Ethan shook his head. "Maybe we should widen the search," Lord Adrian said. "Were all people in the castle checked? I know I wasn't, though you have my word that I didn't find or take the necklace."

"I'll talk to Captain Stuart tomorrow morning. I'm very tired now and, honestly, a little disappointed. I really hoped Daniel would find it right away. It seemed like such an easy task when he came up with the idea."

Bess's coach rattled up a mountain road. He looked out of the window, but his view was blocked by a crag. Suddenly, the rock ended, and a valley appeared. Two high mountains made a breath-taking background to a small town buried in the heart of the valley. The sun was setting, and the valley was much darker than the mountains around the town. Fires were lit in most houses. The lights reminded Bess of stars in a night sky. He leaned out of the coach and looked up at Finn.

"Do you know what town that is?" he asked Finn.

Finn looked at the town and shook his head. "No, but we can't be too far away from Royal City."

"Great," Bess said evenly. He looked at the town. "Please stop the coach," he said to Finn.

Finn pulled on the reins, and the coach stopped. He fixed the reins on the seat and jumped down at the same time Bess opened the door of the coach and stepped outside.

Bess looked at the town and stepped closer to Finn. "I want you to find yourself lodgings for tonight and then return to Wolfast with the coach," he told Finn. "Go via a different road to avoid the guards we met when we came here. Norene guards will most likely let you walk through, so you should have no trouble. They probably mind people going in, not coming out, and the coach doesn't contain anything suspicious."

"What about you?"

"I will continue towards Royal City on my own. I don't want to linger. As a wolf I can run much faster."

"What if someone recognizes that you're a werewolf?"

"I'll keep low and travel as wolf only at night. Then I will try to get a horse somewhere. Don't tell anyone about me. If someone asks, make up something but avoid mentioning Wolfast."

"Don't worry, Bess," Finn said with a smile.

Bess nodded and stepped back. "Good luck," he said, and he watched Finn jump onto the seat of the coach.

"Good luck to you," Finn said with a smile. "You'll need it more than I," he added, and he urged the horses to walk along.

The coach continued on the narrow road until it vanished in the distance. Bess looked around and smelled the air. He was alone. Animals could smell him from far away and choose other paths to avoid him, and humans were probably already at home, eating their evening meals. Time to speed up things.

Bess walked behind a bush and pulled a small bag from his pocket. It was made of a light material and had a simple handle so he could easily carry the bag in his wolf jaws. He knew that a wolf carrying a bag looked suspicious, but he counted on his excellent hearing and smell to avoid people.

He looked around and sniffed the air again. He was still alone. He stripped down as fast as he could. Shaking slightly, partially because of the cold night breeze and partially of excitement, he pushed the clothes into the bag and tied it tight. Then he changed.

He still wasn't completely used to the change. It felt weird. There wasn't any pain involved, just a strange feeling as his body changed shape. The feeling usually remained for a while even after the change was complete. He shook the feeling off and picked up the bag with his teeth. Carefully, he stepped from behind the bush, sniffing the air. He didn't smell anyone. He looked around, checking the up-wind direction thoroughly. He couldn't be a hundred percent sure that he was there alone, but he was pretty certain.

He couldn't linger. He had said that he would do anything to stop Rex, and now he had to risk his life and the truce with Norene to fulfil that promise. He took a deep breath and sprinted up the road. As he ran the first mile, he was full of excitement and adrenalin. By the second mile, he was calming down. It was the middle of the night in the dark forest. People had awful night vision and were loud. He would spot them miles away. The rest of the run was very uneventful. Animals were avoiding Bess at all costs. This made the country quiet and still.

Bess was thrilled when daylight broke above the horizon. He stopped once again, turned back into his human form, and dressed as fast as he could. He had yet to figure out how to change back and forth efficiently. He had been a werewolf for only a few months, so he felt rather clumsy about it.

His head spun a little as he walked towards another village. He was glad he had been able to find the village so quickly and even gladder when he met a farmer who was leading three horses into a pasture.

"Good morning," Bess called at him.

The man jumped, startled, and spun around, looking for the source of the call. When he spotted Bess, he calmed down a little. The horses became nervous and started to neigh. "Good morning to you, too," the farmer said, patting the nearest horse absentmindedly. "It's a very early morning if I may say so."

"Tell me about it! I travelled nearly all night, and when I laid down nearby to rest, I didn't tie my horse properly, and it ran away into the darkness. I need to get to the city quickly, so I would like to buy one of your horses. I can offer you two hundred coins for it."

"Two hundred!" the farmer shouted. The second horse tried to rise up onto its hind legs. "Oh, didn't mean to startle them," he said with a chuckle, and he patted the horse without even looking at it. "But that's a lot of money. These horses aren't worth that much."

"How much do you want for one of them?" Bess asked, aware of the fact the horses were nervous because of him. He needed to seal this deal quickly before the farmer got suspicious.

"Fifty would be good enough for me."

"All right, fifty it is," Bess said, pulling coins from his pouch and counting out fifty of them. When he stopped in an inn in the north of

Wolfast, he had managed to change Wolfast money for Norene money. He didn't know he would have to buy a horse; he just didn't want to take his chances. And since people by the borders traded with the other side, he had no trouble obtaining the required money.

The farmer took the coins and counted them. When he seemed satisfied, he handed Bess the reins. "Here you go," he said with a smile.

Bess smiled and took the reins. He walked up to the horse while the farmer put the coins into a bag on his belt. The horse neighed and stepped back, but Bess was ready for this, and he grabbed the reins tight.

"Why are you in such a hurry?" the farmer asked. The horse neighed some more but let Bess stroke its head.

"I'm supposed to be in Royal City by noon," Bess said and jumped onto the horse. There was no saddle, but this didn't bother Bess. As a boy he had ridden a lot without a saddle. It wasn't very comfortable, but it was manageable. "Any idea where I can buy a saddle?" he asked, just in case. The farmer shook his head, watching him intently. The other two horses moved as far away from Bess as they could. The farmer looked at the horses and then back at Bess.

"Royal City is far away," the farmer said. "You won't make it by noon, even with a saddle and a fast horse. You would have to be a bloody werewolf to run that far that fast." It took all Bess's willpower not to look at the farmer at that moment. He wasn't sure if it was just a statement or if the farmer was suspicious, but quickly looking at him would confirm whatever hypothesis the farmer had.

"I should hurry up then," Bess said, and only then did he look at the farmer. The farmer watched him intently, narrowing his eyes. "Thank you very much. Have a nice day," Bess added with a smile, and he hurried off towards the city. He didn't dare to look over his shoulder, but he could feel the farmer's stare on his back all the way.

The sun was getting very low over Royal City. Christine lay still on the bed in her flat, looking at the ceiling. She yawned and turned onto her belly. She rested her head on her hands and looked at the door. The day before, she had returned home and just gone to bed. She hadn't gotten up since then. She had been ordered to take two days off! What an insult. As if she couldn't do her job properly!

She stood up and walked into the living room. She stopped and looked at the entrance door. This was where she had spoken to John for the last time. She sighed and turned around. Her reflection in the mirror greeted her. She looked awful—dishevelled, shadows beneath her eyes, and a pale face.

Suddenly, a wave of anger flushed over her. She'd never let anyone make her feel sad! Never before! Now she was sad and, on top of that, it was all because of a man! They had known each other only a few days. She hadn't even liked John in the beginning, and now she had stayed in bed for nearly two days because of him. She should have used that time to do something about Rex and the Masked Man. Instead, she had pitied herself. No! No more!

Five minutes later, she marched outside, fully dressed with a purpose in her mind. She had wasted two days. Now it was time to take some action. She would even contact Captain Stuart, the man she despised.

She stopped in front of the Royal Guards' city headquarters and looked at the building. It was two stories taller than the rest of the buildings in the street, which gave it a towering look. She lifted her chin and walked up the stairs into the main hall. A guard sat behind a table, hunched over paperwork. She was glad that it was a different guard than the one she had met at headquarters before.

He looked up. "Is there any trouble, miss?" he asked and stood up.

"I need to talk to Captain Stuart right away," Christine said as confidently as she could.

"Captain Stuart is at the castle. There's some sort of gathering there, and he's overseeing the security," the guard said, and he put down the quill. "Can I be of service?"

"No, I really need Captain Stuart."

"You could go up to the castle, but I'm not sure if he would have time to see you. He's currently overseeing the king's security, you see."

Christine stood still for a while, thinking hard. She really needed to drop all the information on Captain Stuart and let him deal with it. It hadn't even occurred to her that he wouldn't be there.

"When is he coming back?" she asked quietly.

"I'm not sure," the guard said. "He's been living at the castle. He comes into the city only occasionally. You can try and go to see him, or I can call the lieutenant for you. He's going to the castle also."

"That's all right," Christine said, her throat getting tight. She forced a smile and hurried out of the building before she lost her self-control.

She stopped on the street and took a deep breath. She felt disappointed. She had really hoped she would succeed. Both people she wanted to talk to were at the castle—the king and the captain of the Royal Guards. Maybe if she went up there, she could talk to both of them, but she was in no mood to walk the distance at dusk. Soon night would fall, and the castle was too far away.

She turned to the streets of the city, not paying any attention to the darkening sky. She realized that she couldn't go to the king and the captain at that moment, but there was another guy to whom she would like to talk even more. The only trouble was, she had no idea where the Masked Man was hiding.

Daniel and Lord Charles stood in front of a mirror in Lord Charles's room. Daniel was looking at himself in the mirror, tilting his head to his left. He was wearing black trousers and a black shirt, a white shawl. A dark-grey wolf mask covered his face. The mask was even partially covering his eyes. "I don't understand," he said slowly, turning to Lord Charles. "My fur is white when I change, not black."

"The point is not for you to be another version of you," Lord Charles said patiently. "The point is to be someone else completely."

"Why?" Daniel asked as Lord Charles put on the jacket of a ship's captain.

"It's a human thing," Lord Charles said absentmindedly, buttoning his shirt. "You look good like this," he added without even looking at Daniel.

Daniel shrugged and looked at his reflection once more. Then he walked to the anteroom and stopped on the spot. Lucy stood in the middle of the room dressed in a white long robe. She wore small wings on the back of her dress and a white hat with some feathers. She was beautiful. Her long red hair was hidden underneath the hat, and her milky skin blended with the dress.

"Wow," he said with his mouth gapped open.

"Thank you," Lucy said with a smile, and she spun around on the spot. "I like it myself. What do you think I'm supposed to be?"

"Ehm … " Daniel hesitated, not sure what she wanted to hear. "A young woman?"

Lucy laughed merrily as she shook her head. "No," she said kindly. "I'll give you a hint. I'm an animal."

"Humans are animals, aren't they?"

"Yes," Lucy said with laughter, "but I meant my mask. It's supposed to represent an animal—another animal, not a human animal."

"Oh!" It finally dawned on Daniel what she was saying. He looked at the dress. There was a layer of feathers on the skirt. "A goose!" he said happily.

Lucy's smile flicked, but it quickly returned with laughter. "No, I'm a dove," she explained, and she spun around once again so Daniel could have a better look.

"Well, they're not as tasty, but they're still nice," he said with a shrug. Lucy burst out laughing. Daniel didn't understand what was so funny.

"I like your mask," Lucy said, motioning towards Daniel clothes. He looked down at his chest. "Didn't you want to go as something else? After all, you are a wolf."

"Why does everyone say that?"

"Never mind that," Lucy said. She waved her hand dismissively. A breeze from the window reached her skirt and played with some of the feathers. "You look lovely. It suits you."

"Thanks," Daniel said with a smile, not sure if Lucy meant that comment as a good thing. Then he smelled a woman's scent from the window. He sniffed the air and slowly walked towards the open window.

"What's wrong?" Lucy asked with concern in her voice.

"I can smell the same woman who broke into my room back home. She's here. She's in the castle."

"Are you sure it's the same woman?"

"Yes! I first smelled her in this very castle right before we met the werewolves and I ran into the burning store house. That's how I remembered the smell when she came to visit me at home. It was definitely the same woman. And now I smell her again. She's here."

"Who is she?" Lucy asked. She sounded a little scared. She stood against the breeze so Daniel couldn't smell her mood, but he was getting better at guessing human emotions from the tone of voices and expressions on the faces.

"I have no idea," Daniel said with a shrug, and he carefully leaned out of the window. He looked around. The scent lingered in the air, but he couldn't see anyone. The sun was setting, leaving the halo of twilight in the sky, which illuminated the castle. If there was someone out there, she would be completely visible. Daniel couldn't imagine how anyone could be hiding in that light.

"Maybe we should inform someone?" Lucy asked nervously.

Daniel didn't want to waste time with humans at the moment. They would want all sorts of information, and meanwhile the woman could get away. Therefore, he didn't even respond to the suggestion. Instead, he spun around and bolted towards the corridor just as Lord Charles entered the anteroom.

"Inform someone about what?" Daniel heard him ask just as he entered the corridor. The only thing that mattered to him at the moment was the scent of the mysterious woman. The scent lingered for a moment in the air, but then it vanished. Daniel stopped. His feet slid down the marble floor, and then he came to a complete halt.

He looked around, surprised. He hadn't expected the scent to just vanish. There were many scents in the corridor, including those of some sweaty men. Daniel expected the woman's scent to linger, but it was useless. All he could smell was men's sweat. He hesitated. Maybe he couldn't follow the scent now, but he was sure that it would pop up in some other part of the castle.

He looked over his shoulder at the corridor he had just come from. In the distance, he could see the door to their quarters. Maybe if he went back, he could tell Lord Charles what had happened. He hung his head low and turned back, walking slowly, one foot in front of the other. Then he caught the scent once again. He sniffed the air and followed the scent all the way to the door of the room. He stopped, feeling discouraged. It was the same trail he had already followed.

He heard Lord Charles's voice inside the room, though he couldn't understand the actual words. He stood in front of the door, thinking hard.

He was very curious about the trail. Why had it appeared in their room all of a sudden? Had the woman used their room to get inside the castle or to escape? He watched the door for a while and then decided to check the stairs. He stepped away, walking slowly. The scents were too mixed up in the corridor for Daniel to understand them.

Suddenly, chills ran down his spine. All his senses screamed, and the hair on the back of his neck stood up. He looked up at the ceiling, not really seeing it. It felt as if the necklace was calling to him from the floor above. He stepped towards the stairs and then broke into run. He reached the landing feeling as if something bad was about to happen or had already happened. He reached the top of the stairs and continued down the corridor.

He sprinted by the library and stopped. He spun around and sniffed the air. The scent was very weak, but it was still distinguishable in the air even amongst other scents of all the people around him. The scent of the necklace was stronger in here—or the scent of someone who had held the necklace not long ago.

He sniffed the air and followed the scent into the library. There was no one in the library, but the scent lingered. It was mixed with some other scents, but not so many as were in the corridors. There were both female and male scents, but Daniel recognized Lord James's and Ethan's amongst them. This could mean that he was sniffing the remnants of the necklace's scent from Ethan. Daniel sighed. He had really been hopeful for a moment. It seemed like he might actually be able to find the necklace after all. Then again, this scent was too strong to have been several days old.

"What's going on?" a voice asked from the door. Daniel spun around. Lord James stood on the threshold with his arms folded, watching Daniel intently. He was dressed normally, not wearing a mask.

"Intruder," Daniel explained.

Lord James froze. Then he blinked. He looked around the empty library. "I think I need more information," he said.

"A woman," Daniel said.

"Even more information," Lord James said calmly.

Daniel looked around as he sniffed the air. "A woman attacked me back home," he said. "I smelled her just a few moments ago in here. She's in the castle. I don't know who she is, but I think she's dangerous. I think she's after the necklace."

"Have you seen her? Now or before? Do you know what she looks like?"

Daniel sighed. He was right. The humans always wanted so much information before they started to act! "No, not really," he said. "She attacked me in Leurn, but it was too dark to see. But the scent doesn't change with the light. I know it's her."

"I would never doubt your nose," Lord James said. "It's just that the guards can't search for someone based on the scent. We humans don't have that ability."

"Oh," Daniel said as he understood Lord James's point of view. "No, I haven't seen her. But she wore dark clothes. She hides in shadows, so maybe we need to check every dark corner and dark room."

Lord James looked at Daniel and then scanned the library. "Thanks for the information," he said, and he spun around. Before Daniel managed to say anything, Lord James was out of the library.

Daniel stood still for a moment, frowning after Lord James. He wasn't sure if the expression "Thanks for the information" was supposed to mean something to him. Maybe he could ask Lord James what he meant by that. He stepped outside the library. Lord James was already farther down the corridor, telling something to a guard. The guard listened intently. Then he saluted and sprinted away.

Lord James looked around, and when he spotted a perplexed Daniel, he stepped towards him. "Go to the ball and don't worry about this," Lord James told him. "I'll take care of everything with Captain Stuart. If you hear or see—or smell—anything unusual, tell any guard you meet. Don't worry. We'll sort this out." He looked Daniel up and down, his gaze stopping on the mask on Daniel's face. "Nice mask, by the way," he said with a smile. "I would have thought you'd choose something other than a wolf, though," he added, and he left Daniel standing in the corridor.

Daniel looked down at his clothes and shrugged. He was no longer curious about why everyone was telling him he was a wolf; now he was curious only about the scent. He was in no mood to go to a masquerade. He wanted to find the woman or the necklace.

He spun around, returned to the library, and sniffed the air again. Suddenly, the very strong scent of male sweat reached his nose and cancelled any possibility of smelling anything else. He turned to the front door and looked at a guard at the threshold.

"Is everything all right?" the guard asked Daniel. Daniel nodded vigorously. The guard hesitated and then nodded at Daniel and left the library. The scent lingered.

Daniel pulled the mask off his face and looked around. He had two options. He could wait for the guard's scent to become less obvious and then use his nose to search for the woman, or he could search for her without using his nose. He wasn't used to the second option, so he just sat down with his back to the wall and watched the library like a hawk. He had a feeling that the woman was hiding there somewhere. He just needed to wait for her to show herself, or for his senses to get better.

CHAPTER 7

Ethan walked up to the ballroom in the castle, adjusting the black panther mask on the way. He had given specific orders that his presence was not to be acknowledged in any special way, and he hoped that the music wouldn't stop in respect for him when he entered the hall. He just wanted to have a nice evening, and he wanted everyone else to have a nice evening.

He entered the hall and stopped by the door. There were some people he didn't recognize. The masks made it even more difficult. People were either standing by the walls or dancing in the middle of the room. Ethan spotted Lady Joan. She was dancing with Lord Adrian. Lord Charles was also on the dance floor, dancing with Mary. And Lucy was dancing with Lieutenant Ernest nearby.

Ethan turned his attention to Lady Joan. She was dressed as Goddess Beatrice, the goddess of love. She wore a beautiful white dress with wide skirts and a white diadem on her head. She looked radiant. Lord Adrian was dressed like a priest of old.

Lord Adrian noticed Ethan and nodded to him. Lady Joan looked over her shoulder and flashed Ethan a smile. Ethan tried to smile back, but he felt nervous. He nodded and quickly turned away. He spotted a table of food in the corner. There were more people there. King Philip's former advisor, Brian, was talking to a guard at the one end of the table, and Lord Thomas was putting food on a plate at the other.

Ethan walked over to Lord Thomas, trying to figure out what he was dressed as. It took him a while, but in the end, he figured out that he was supposed to be a bear. A fur coat covered his big belly, which seemed even bigger after his month-long visit with the troops, and a fake bear nose on a string was hanging around his neck. There was a strange hairy thing lying on the table, which Ethan took for part of the costume—probably a hat to cover Lord Thomas's bald head. It was the same colour as his chestnut beard.

"Good evening, My Lord," Ethan said with a smile as he stopped next to him. "Enjoying yourself?"

"Oh, good evening, Your Majesty," Lord Thomas said with a smile and a small bow of his head. "I think this was a great idea," he said, and he waved the fork in his hand in the direction of the dance floor.

"I hope you're staying till the end."

"Of course. I wouldn't have missed this for the world. I even gave my staff the day off, and Lord Adrian prepared a room for me in the castle. I plan to enjoy the evening. You have an excellent wine here. And the food's delicious. You should try it."

"Good idea," Ethan said as he picked up a plate. He looked at the food and hesitated. "What would you recommend?"

"I love these small cakes," Lord Thomas said. With his fork, he pointed to a plate of bite-sized cakes in front of Ethan. "I could eat hundreds of them. And this ham is delicious. It's so light and well smoked."

Ethan picked up one cake and tasted it. It was really good, but he was in no mood to taste another one. He was too nervous at the moment. "How's your family?" he asked Lord Thomas. "Aren't they coming?"

"No. My wife regrets that she can't be here, but she wanted to stay near our daughter-in-law. Our son got married last year, and they're expecting a baby any time now."

"So you'll be a grandfather," Ethan said with a smile.

"Yes. I can't wait. I'm actually going back home in two days."

The music stopped, and Ethan quickly looked at Lord Adrian, who bowed to Lady Joan and then gently led her towards the table with food. Ethan put the plate down and stepped forward. He had to act now before all the courage left him. Lord Thomas looked after him, obviously curious.

Ethan stopped in front of Lady Joan, who was smiling radiantly at him. "May I have this next dance?" he asked nervously, offering her his hand. She nodded and took his hand. He felt like dancing and singing at that moment. He lifted his head and led Lady Joan onto the dance floor. Most of the people in the room were watching them. Lord Adrian was smiling brightly, Lord Thomas looked a little surprised, and Mary looked disappointed.

Ethan turned his focus on Lady Joan. He had been dreaming of this dance ever since he came up with the idea of a ball, and now, when he finally held her in his arms, he felt that none of his dreams could beat reality. She was so light on her feet and so much at ease with him that his heart calmed down. He enjoyed every moment.

"Thank you so much for inviting me here," Lady Joan said with a bright smile. "It's been such a lovely evening. My whole stay has been wonderful. I never felt so at home anywhere before."

"I'm glad you like it here."

"I love it here. The library is magnificent, and the horses are beautiful. And, of course, your presence improves on the place hugely. Your servants are very fond of you, and they try hard to make the palace feel comfortable." Ethan could feel his cheeks burning. He felt so lightheaded. "Your father would have been proud of you for all that you have achieved in such a short time. I'm sorry I never had the privilege of meeting your father," Lady Joan said, and her smile vanished for a while. "I remember him as a great man and king."

"He was also a great father. I miss him every day," Ethan confessed.

"The old monks used to believe that people never really leave us even after death. They believe that the dead stay behind as ghosts and look after us. I don't believe that. I don't think anyone does today. But I think that there is some truth in that belief. People we love never really leave us. They live in our memories. And when we feel down or scared, that's when they are closest to us. Maybe it's a superstition, but I like to think that my mum still lives inside me. And one day I will tell my children about her, and she will live on through those stories."

"Nicely put," Ethan said.

"Thank you," Lady Joan said with a smile. Then she hung her head, and a chilly sadness radiated towards Ethan. "I'll miss this place," she said.

"I hope you're not thinking of leaving," Ethan said as calmly as he could. Panic rose inside him.

"I've taken advantage of your hospitality long enough," Lady Joan said without looking at Ethan. "It's time for me to go back home." Ethan stopped, still holding Lady Joan close to him. Lady Joan looked at him surprised. "The music's still playing," she said, confused.

He watched her intently, thinking hard. Then he made his decision. He had to do something he had wanted to do for some time now—he only now realized it. "I need to talk to you," he said as he took her hand. He led her outside the ballroom and onto the balcony over the main gate, ignoring curious stares. They were alone there. Ethan stopped far away from the ballroom and turned to face a perplexed Lady Joan. With his free hand, he pulled off the mask off his face. "I've enjoyed your company immensely," he said, still holding her hand. "I don't know what the future will bring, but I feel less afraid of it when I'm with you."

Lady Joan watched him with huge eyes. She blushed and smiled nervously. Then she cleared her throat. "I can't pretend that I don't fancy you," she said in nearly a whisper. "But I would never even dare to dream that you fancied me."

"I fell for you the minute I saw you. And the more I got to know you, the more I cared for you. That's why … " he took a deep breath and knelt down on one knee. He had expected the gasp Lady Joan made. He had even expected that she would cover her mouth with her free hand, but he hadn't expected that she would look terrified. Then she started to cry.

"I can't," she said with a sob, before he could say anything more. She freed her hand and shook her head. "Please, don't ask me!" And with that, she ran off the balcony, leaving Ethan kneeling on the cold stone. His feeling of complete happiness changed to bewilderment and then to anger. He had no idea what had just happened, and he was in no mood to try to find it out. He stood up and looked at the crowded hall. It seemed that there had been no witnesses to his humiliation. He didn't want to see anyone or talk to anyone. For a brief moment, he had thought that he was the luckiest man in Norene. Now he was just the biggest fool.

He put his mask back on to cover his embarrassment and left the balcony. He sneaked through the ballroom and walked to his office, ignoring the salutes of the guards. When he closed the door of his office behind him, he leaned against it and softly banged his head against the heavy wood until it hurt. At least the headache made the pain in his chest less obvious. He sighed and marched to the table.

He pulled the mask off his face and threw it onto the desk. He was tempted to throw everything off the desk. He picked up a book and threw it with all his might against the wall by the window. It hit the stone and fell to the floor. He then grabbed another book, ready to send it after the first one. Then he froze. The last person throwing things in this office had been Mors, just before Ethan had killed him. That memory calmed Ethan down. He looked down at the book in his hands. There were worse things than being rejected by the woman he loved. Being dead was on the top of the list. Losing his kingdom would also be worse. Watching his friends die was excruciating. So why did Lady Joan's rejection hurt so much now?

"A rough night?" a man asked behind Ethan in a hoarse whisper. Ethan spun around, prepared to throw the book at whoever stood there. By the wall, close to the closed door, there stood a tall man in a mask and wearing a hat. Ethan immediately recognized the hat. He knew the voice. The figure matched too. This was the Masked Man. Right now, Ethan was in no mood to talk to him.

"You've no idea," he said, and he put the book down. He walked around the table and sat down. He felt better there, knowing that his sword was beneath the table.

"Trust me, I have," the Masked Man said. "I wish I could help you in the matter."

"Thanks, but I'm not sure how you could," Ethan said annoyed. He was in no mood to deal with anyone, especially with the guy who was possibly a criminal. Maybe Ethan should have called the guards right away. He even wondered why he hadn't done so yet. "What do you want?" he snapped at the Masked Man. "I doubt you came here to console me."

"I'm still looking for the necklace. And from what I hear, I'm not the only one. I came to ask if you have any idea where it is. Please, let me take it away."

"I wish I could," Ethan said quietly. "I would give you the wretched thing gladly, but it has vanished. Even Daniel can't find it. And you know what? I don't care anymore. It's out of my hands, and I hope it will stay away forever."

"I hope so too," the Masked Man said in a whisper, the hoarseness of his voice momentarily vanishing. It felt like an honest answer. Ethan looked at the Masked Man. The man bowed his head and left the room via the door. He closed the door behind him, leaving Ethan alone. Ethan wasn't sure whether to feel relieved or sad. He put his head into his hands and sighed. How could have he been happy before? Happiness now felt like a completely forgotten emotion.

He thought of going to bed, but he couldn't find enough energy to stand up. Maybe he should have called the guards and informed them of the presence of the Masked Man, but even that required energy.

Suddenly, the door flew open. Ethan jumped to his feet, reaching for his sword, but then he froze. Lady Joan, tears running down her cheeks, ran towards him. He watched her as she reached him and threw her arms around his neck. He hugged her back, completely lost for words. He stroked her hair, as she wept on his shoulder. They stood there for a while, Lady Joan sobbing, and Ethan completely bewildered and unable to find any words. Then clicks in the corridor reached Ethan's ears over Lady Joan's sobs. He knew right away that Captain Stuart was coming. Ethan looked at the door as the captain entered, followed by a few guards. The captain was a little pale but resolute.

"What's going on?" Ethan asked the captain.

"There's been a murder," Captain Stuart said quietly. He looked at Lady Joan and then back at Ethan. "Lady Joan's maid was killed in Lady Joan's quarters. Someone stabbed her and forced a jewellery box open."

Ethan looked at the weeping woman in his arms and gently pushed her into the chair. He knelt down next to her and asked as kindly as he could, "Joan, did you have my necklace?"

Lady Joan nodded with a sob. "I found it two days ago—late in the evening." She hiccoughed. "I put it in my jewellery box and then completely forgot ab—about it. I wanted to give it to you the—the next morning, but it slipped my mind. I didn't remember the necklace until now when I saw—" a wail followed these words.

Ethan waited patiently for Lady Joan to compose herself. He exchanged looks with Captain Stuart, who stood by the open door with a few guards. Ethan looked into the corridor, wondering where the Masked Man had gone. He turned back to Lady Joan, who was finally calming down. She hiccoughed and looked at Ethan. "I quickly checked the jewellery box, and your necklace was the only thing—" Ethan only guessed that the last word was *missing* because that was when Lady Joan issued another wail. She buried her face in her handkerchief.

Ethan looked at Captain Stuart and stood up. "I suppose that someone found it," he said, wondering why the Masked Man had come to him when he already had the necklace. Unless …

"Daniel informed Lord James of a woman in the castle," Captain Stuart said. "Someone who wasn't supposed to be here. He said that she attacked him in Leurn in his room. Lord James got some guards and searched the castle. He also informed me right away. I sent more men to the ball to keep an eye on the guests. The rest of the men are searching the castle. The guards were on the fourth floor, searching every room when Lady Joan returned to her quarters. Her scream immediately summoned my men. If she had gone to her room two minutes later, they would have been checking her quarters and would have found the maid. I'm sorry we didn't manage to stop her from discovering the body herself."

"Did you find out something about the attacker afterwards?"

"No. We don't know who attacked the maid, but I think it was the woman Daniel smelled in the castle. That or—"

"The Masked Man," Ethan finished Captain Stuart's sentence himself. Then he scratched the idea. If the Masked Man had murdered the maid and stolen the necklace, he wouldn't have paid Ethan a visit. And there hadn't been enough time for the Masked Man to commit the murder after their meeting. Lady Joan had run into his office soon after the Masked Man had left. "No, it had to be the woman Daniel smelled," Ethan said resolutely. "But how would she know where to look?"

"Maybe the maid mentioned the necklace to someone," Captain Stuart said. "We were searching for it, but not amongst the guests. The servants were bound to discuss any mention of it."

"Search the castle and inform me at once," Ethan said to Captain Stuart, who saluted and left the office. The guards followed him, closing the door behind them. Ethan was suddenly alone with Lady Joan. He looked at her and then knelt down. He looked up into her face. She was still beautiful, even with red watery eyes.

"I owe you an explanation," she whispered, and she hiccoughed. Ethan shook his head. "I mean about the proposal," she added.

"Oh, that," Ethan said. His stomach vanished. No good conversation ever started with words "I owe you an explanation".

"Nothing would make me happier than being able to say yes," Lady Joan said, "but I think that you came to wrong conclusions about me. When I came here, I said that I was Lord Eric's granddaughter. This is true, but you probably thought that meant that I am a lady. I'm not. I have no right to that title because my mother was Lord Eric's illegitimate child. I never said I was a lady, and I asked you to not call me that, but I think that you still believed that I'm someone I'm not."

Ethan blinked. "Why didn't you say something sooner?" he asked, stunned.

"I was afraid you would be mad," Lady Joan confessed, tears running down her cheeks. "I didn't mean to lead you on. I fancied you from the beginning, and this way I had an excuse to stay close, though I didn't deserve your hospitality. I was so thrilled when you asked me to stay for the summer. I hadn't dared to think that you fancied me. If I had, I would have left."

"Why did you stay?" Ethan asked, trying to keep his voice calm. Anger was bubbling inside him.

"I don't know," Joan whispered. "I guess I thought I could gain something," she admitted.

Ethan stood up and folded his arms. He wasn't sure what to say to this. He wasn't sure what was worse—her refusal of his offer or her explanation for why she said no in the first place. Joan looked up at him, obviously waiting for him to say something. Rage filled him. He was king, and he had been deceived so easily! And he had actually liked her so much before all of this happened!

He spun on his heel and barged out of the office. He slammed the door behind him and walked up the corridor. He had taken only a few steps when he spotted an open window nearby. He walked up to it and looked outside. The sun had set already, and the castle and the yard were quite dark. Ethan spun around, and his gaze fell on a wolf mask on the floor by the wall. This was not one of the castle masks. He picked it up and looked at it. He would have sworn that this was the same mask the Masked Man had worn in Ethan's office. Ethan looked at the door of his office and then at the window. The Masked Man could have heard the conversation amongst Joan, Ethan, and Captain Stuart. He was now probably after the mysterious woman the captain had mentioned.

"Your Majesty," Lord Charles said behind him. Ethan spun around, startled. He hadn't heard Lord Charles coming. Lord Charles opened his mouth to talk, but when he saw Ethan's expression, he hesitated. "Are you all right?" he asked.

"Yes," Ethan said, and he threw the mask to the ground. "Never better," he snapped and looked out of the window again.

"Have you seen Daniel?" Lord Charles asked. "I haven't seen him all evening."

Ethan looked at Lord Charles's worried face. "He's probably somewhere in the castle," he said.

Lord Charles looked down the corridor. "I thought so too," he said nervously, "but it's been a long time. The last time I saw him was right before the ball. When I came to the anteroom, he ran outside. Lucy said that he had smelled something strange. I just hope he didn't get himself into some trouble."

Ethan didn't want to deal with the Masked Man or the dead maid, and he definitely didn't want to hear anything about Joan. Looking for Daniel would be a great opportunity to avoid everything. "Let's search for him," he said, and he walked towards the stairs.

"Shouldn't you go back to the masquerade?" Lord Charles asked as he followed Ethan. Ethan stopped and slowly turned to face him. He looked at Lord Charles, until Lord Charles shrugged. "They can do without us," Lord Charles said with a wave of his hand.

"Sure they can," Ethan snapped, and he continued down the stairs.

Daniel watched every inch of the library like a hawk. The scent of the guard was getting weaker, but the woman's scent had disappeared altogether. He hesitated. He stood up and started to walk around the room, checking every corner and every shelf.

It took only a fraction of a second, but a breeze washed over his face. When he looked at the window, it was closed, but he wasn't fooled by that for a second. He jumped to the window and immediately smelled the woman. She had been in the library, and now she had left it. What was more startling was the fact he could smell the necklace by the window too.

He spun around and sprinted out of the library and towards the staircase. He was no expert in human behaviour, but he would bet anything that the woman was trying to get out of the castle.

Bess rode out of the forest and stopped the horse. His thighs hurt after an entire day of riding without a saddle. He hadn't wanted to waste his time stopping to buy a saddle, but now he regretted that. He wondered if the journey would have been faster with a saddle, but he made himself believe that the horse ran faster without a saddle to obstruct its movement.

He looked at Royal City in front of him. It was one of the most beautiful cities in the north of Lanland. He hadn't had a chance to see the city properly when he was in Norene the last time, but he had noticed it right away. Even Wolfast's capital faded in comparison. White walls surrounded the buildings behind it. Torches were lit along the whole length of the walls, throwing the city into dimmed light. The buildings were built from the same material as the walls, making the city look bigger from the outside. The stone was light yellow, but it appeared white in the torchlight, and red rooftops created a contrast.

Bess had hoped he would reach the city by noon, but he had obviously underestimated the distance. His original plan had been to go to the castle and demand to see the king, hoping that the guards would let him through, but now that he saw the city and the castle to his far left, he wasn't so sure any more. He wasn't welcome in Norene, and going to the castle so late could be to his disadvantage.

Then he thought of getting some additional information during the night. He didn't need sleep as often as humans did for which he was thankful. He could try to sniff out some information and then go to Ethan in the morning.

He spurred the horse towards the city gate. He was nervous that the guards would stop him and interrogate him, but they merely watched him curiously. He felt this was mostly because he rode a horse without a saddle. He slowed down expecting some questions from the guards, but one of the guards motioned for him to continue. Bess nodded and entered the city, trying to look calm.

He moved away from the gate, hoping to get out of sight of guards, but the city was flooded with the Royal Guards. He stopped in the main square and looked around. There was another bigger group of guards walking slowly through the square, checking the rooftops. Bess watched them curiously. On the one hand, they appeared to be looking for someone. On the other, they were too casual about their task.

Bess jumped down from the horse and nearly collapsed onto the ground. His knees refused to straighten up, and the muscles in his thighs screamed in protest. He used to ride without a saddle when he was a boy, but that had always been only for a few minutes, not for a few hours. He wouldn't have travelled without the saddle for so long if he wasn't a werewolf. As a werewolf, he knew that he would heal within a few hours.

He massaged his thighs, trying to relieve some of the pain. It didn't help. He straightened up, ignoring the pain. Every joint in his body cracked. He took a hesitant step, trying to push the knees together. Still holding the reins, he stepped towards the watering fountain. The horse neighed and followed him, speeding up as they approached the fountain. Bess looked around while he let the horse drink.

A few guards were watching him curiously. Bess got a little nervous. Many of Lord Blake's soldiers had joined the Royal Guards. What if some of them were here now? What if they recognized him?

He noticed a sign on a building, pointing to a narrow street, indicating that the stables were up there. He pulled at the reins, and the horse unwillingly moved away from the water. He led the horse through the square, avoiding the curious stares. He didn't need the horse anymore, so he decided to let him rest for the night.

Daniel followed his nose all the way to the yard. Out there, he started to walk up and down, trying to catch the woman's scent. Normally, he would have more trouble following the trail through the castle and the yard, but the necklace had strong enough scent for Daniel to smell. Daniel wasn't sure if he imagined it, but he had a feeling that the scent was getting stronger. It felt as if the necklace wanted to be found by Daniel. It took Daniel only a second to catch the trail because it overpowered everything else.

He stopped by the ruins of the warehouse and looked around, sniffing the air. The sun had set, and darkness had fallen, but he could see rather well. There was a slim figure on the other side of the burnt remnants of the warehouse. The figure was climbing the castle walls. He tilted his head to the left to have a better look. He wasn't an expert in humans, but this one seemed to be a woman. The figure didn't linger on the walls. As soon as she reached the top, she jumped from his view. Soon afterwards he heard a horse's neigh followed by shouts from the guards on the walls. It seemed the woman had a horse hidden on the other side of the walls.

He didn't need to follow the trail anymore. The woman had to have the necklace, and now she was out of the castle. Daniel sprinted around the warehouse towards the castle walls. He hadn't paid much attention to the courtyard, and he nearly missed more shouts and a man riding a horse out of the castle's stables. The guards on the walls stood still, surprised by everything that was suddenly happening. A sergeant was the first one to gather his wits.

"Fire!" he shouted at the guards, and arrows flew off the walls. Daniel didn't stop as he sprinted towards the castle walls. The scent was still hanging in the air as he climbed onto the platform. He jumped to the outer wall and looked down through the embrasure. The forest was to Daniel's right. Fields stretched out in front of him all the way to Royal City. Down on the fields he saw a man on a horse, speeding away from the castle. His coat was flapping in the wind, and a hat was distinguishable on his head. Daniel spotted the woman farther away from the castle, vanishing into the darkness. Two guards on horses bolted after the man and the woman, and the guards in the castle lifted the bridge.

Daniel didn't care who the man and the woman were. All he wanted was the necklace. He was the one who had found it, and he had given it to Ethan. Therefore, he was the one who should have the last say in the matter. Without much thinking, he began to throw off his clothes. He didn't even wait till he had removed all of them before he started to change. He threw the trousers to the ground and jumped off the castle wall while he was still changing. Though he jumped as mostly a man, he landed in the water of the moat as a wolf. He dove down, hitting the bottom of the moat. He used the ground to kick himself towards the surface. He emerged above the water, taking a deep breath. He heard shouts from the wall, but he ignored them. In two quick moves, he reached the edge of the water and climbed out onto the grassy bank. He shook off the water and bolted after the man on the horse.

"Was that Daniel?" Ethan asked, pointing towards the castle wall. Guards were running towards the place where the strange silhouette had stood. They were shouting at each other and motioning at something on the other side of the wall. Ethan wasn't completely sure what he had seen in the darkness, but was almost sure he'd seen a man turning into a wolf.

"Either that, or there are werewolves here," Lord Charles said nervously.

"Okay. Let's say that it was Daniel."

"Do you think he saw something?"

"Probably," Ethan said, thinking of the mysterious woman.

"I hope he won't do something stupid," Lord Charles said as he spun around. He bolted towards the stables, leaving Ethan temporarily alone by the castle. Ethan looked after Lord Charles and then ran after him. He was in no mood to be left behind.

When they reached the stables, Lord Charles jumped towards the first horse. He grabbed a saddle from the stand by the wall and threw it over the horse's back. A guard jumped towards them, and when he spotted them, he saluted. Lord Charles didn't acknowledge his presence, and Ethan ignored him. He grabbed a saddle and walked to the horse next to Lord Charles's. He threw the saddle over the horse's back and strapped it under the horse's belly.

Lord Charles froze, watching Ethan. "You shouldn't be leaving the castle, Sire," he said.

Ethan turned around and threw him a black look. "The last time I checked, I was the one making decisions," he said coldly. Lord Charles blushed, which was visible even by the lantern light, and busied himself with the horse. Ethan turned to his horse and tightened the girth. The horse neighed in protest and stepped from one foot to another. The guard hurried forward and put a bridle onto the horse, handing the reins to Ethan.

"Give me your sword," Ethan told the guard. The guard looked up in surprise but then quickly untied his belt and handed it to Ethan. Ethan put the belt around his waist as Lord Charles jumped into his saddle.

"Your Majesty," Lord Charles said from the saddle timidly. "I'm not sure what awaits us out there. It might get too dangerous for you—"

"I'm going," Ethan snapped, and he jumped into the saddle. He was fed up with all this fuss around him. Joan's face flashed in front of his eyes, and he spurred the horse hard. The horse neighed in protest and bolted out of the stables. He reached the yard and turned the horse towards the gate.

The guards spotted him right away and quickly lowered the bridge. Ethan looked over his shoulder. Lord Charles was far behind him. He had probably stayed behind to tell the guard to inform someone—Lord James or Captain Stuart—what was going on. This didn't improve Ethan's mood. He was no child, and he could leave the castle when he wanted to! He spurred the horse again and sprinted after Daniel with Lord Charles at his heels.

CHAPTER 8

C hristine turned the corner and reached the north gate of the city walls. There were seven or so guards standing nearby. Christine wondered if these were there as a precaution, or if they were actually looking for someone—the Masked Man, for instance. The north gate was the smallest of all the gates into the city. No carts could fit through the small space between the walls, for it was way too narrow. It was also short, and riders on horseback often had to stoop or dismount before they could go through. Seven guards guarding this small gate seemed like overkill to Christine. There was usually only one guard, two tops.

Christine stopped nearby and watched them curiously. She was tempted to go to them and ask why they were there, but they all seemed a little nervous. She stood there for a minute or so, wondering if other gates were also this heavily guarded. But then the shouts of the guards from the outside the gate reached her. They had spotted someone and were shouting for the person to stop. There were some more shouts, and the guards on the inside side of the gate stopped as well, looking at the gate. Christine sneaked closer to have a better look. She scanned the darkness.

She wasn't sure if it was just her imagination, but the shadows were weird on the other side of the gate. Then she noticed that one shadow was moving. Two guards, illuminated by torches on either side of the gate, stepped in front of the gate, and one of them lifted his palm to stop the approaching shadow. The shadow was approaching fast, and Christine wondered if the guard blocking the gate was brave or suicidal. On the other hand, the other guards were way too calm. The shadow had to be a person on a horse. Anything else would cause the guards to react differently rather than just blocking the way.

The guard who held his hand outstretched screamed and reached for his sword. He moved to the side, but before he could draw the sword or get completely out of the way, the shadow crashed into him, sending him to the ground. His colleague jumped aside just in time. The shadow fell to the ground and separated into to two lumps. Though the shadow fell into the light, it still looked like a dark lump. All the other guards drew their swords and readied themselves. The smaller shadow—a person—jumped up and sprinted through the gate while the bigger shadow—a horse—stood up and ran away into the field. A woman's silhouette emerged on the other side of the gate. Without the slightest hesitation, she bolted towards the streets.

The guards shouted after her, and three even jumped forward, but she slalomed around them briskly. Though they outnumbered her significantly, none of them was able to stop her. Christine hardly noticed the woman's movement as the woman vanished in the darkness. The two guards from the front of the gate rushed into the city, their swords ready. The guard who had crashed with the shadow was bleeding from his forehead. He was white as a sheet, breathing rapidly, but otherwise he looked unharmed. Most of the guards sprinted after the mysterious woman, leaving only two surprised guards by the gate—the one who had tried to stop the woman with the hand gesture and another who seemed way too young to be a guard already.

Christine hesitated and then stepped after the woman. Suddenly, she heard a horse neigh in the distance. She looked over her shoulder at the gate and noticed another moving shadow out of the corner of her eye. She looked up and could have sworn that a shadow flew from one roof to another. She was sure that it was the Masked Man. Without any hesitation, she sprinted after the shadow, trying to avoid the guards in the streets.

After two turns, she realized that she was no match for the Masked Man. There was no way she could keep up with him on the ground while he was jumping from one roof to another. She stopped, fighting for her breath. Guards were running up and down the street, ignoring her. She wondered if the guards who ran after the woman had raised the alarm. She had never seen this many guards in the city before. An hour ago, they had been calmly walking the streets, checking the shadows and hidden places. Now, they were running through the streets. Christine half expected the woman to be arrested already.

Christine finally caught her breath. She straightened up and looked at the roof where she had spotted the Masked Man last. There was no point in running after him. She stood no chance. She had to figure out where he was headed. An image of the old warehouse appeared in her mind. She had no way of knowing if that was where he was going, but it was the only place she had connected with the Masked Man. That was also the place where she had seen the woman in black clothes. It was a wild guess, but she would wager that the shadow of the woman running through the gate and the woman in the old warehouse were the same person.

Christine swirled and sprinted into one of the hidden alleyways; it was a shortcut through the city. When she reached the other end, she spotted a silhouette on the roof jumping from one roof to another. She knew right away it had to be the Masked Man. He had successfully leaped across a huge gap, but for the Masked Man it was no trouble. Feeling encouraged by the fact she had found him so quickly, she sprinted towards another alleyway farther up the street. She ran into the alley, looking at the rooftops. She ran out into a square and stopped, fighting for her breath. She cursed and grabbed her side. She looked around, trying to ignore the pain.

The square was rather busy, considering the late hour. Some guards were in the square talking to a group of people. Christine walked towards the centre of the square and looked at the rooftops. She couldn't see the Masked Man anywhere. If he wanted to get to the old warehouse, he would have to either walk the rooftops around the huge square or sprint through the centre of the square with all the guards present. This was her chance to catch up with the Masked Man.

She bolted through the square, ignoring the pain in her side. She stopped only when she reached the other side. She was hoping that one of the buildings had a yard that was open on the other side. Suddenly, a strange noise reached her ears.

She listened to the silence of the night, panting. Voices from the middle of the square were the only thing she could hear. She was wondering where the previous sound had come from when she remembered a dead-end alley between the houses. She sprinted towards the gate that blended in with the façade. As usual, the gate was unlocked, and she opened it. She hurried deeper inside and stopped when she heard a crash.

There was a fight going on inside. She carefully approached two fighting silhouettes at the end of the alley. Quickly, she hid behind a wall of cut wood that was stacked by the wall. She glanced over the top. The Masked Man was fighting the woman she'd seen at the gate. The woman held something glittery in her hand as she swung her arm at the Masked Man. The Masked Man leaned back, avoided the thing—which was, in Christine's opinion, a knife—and managed to grab her wrist. He punched the back of her hand hard, and the woman screamed, opening her hand.

There was a nasty cracking noise, and the knife flew towards Christine, clanging in the darkness. Both the Masked Man and the woman completely ignored the fallen knife. The Masked Man let go of the woman's hand and grabbed her by her throat. He lifted her up and smashed her against the wall of the house, tightening his grip on her throat.

"Stop this, Amy," he said hoarsely as Amy choked in his grip. "Give me the necklace, and I will let you go."

Amy wasn't going to give up so easily. She kicked at the Masked Man, but the kick was too weak for him to notice. Amy grabbed his hand and tried to pull free, but his hold was too strong. Then she rapidly outstretched her fingers and jabbed at the Masked Man's throat. The move was so fast that Christine nearly missed it. Maybe even the Masked Man would have missed it if Amy hadn't managed to hit him precisely in his suprasternal notch. The Masked Man coughed and released Amy. Amy fell heavily onto the ground, but she used the momentum and kicked at the Masked Man's groin as he staggered back. The Masked Man saw the blow coming. He grabbed her foot in mid-air and twisted. Amy took advantage of his hold on her. She spun around, kicking at his head with her free leg.

Her shin landed on the side of his face, throwing him to the side. He let go of her and staggered, his hat falling to the ground. Amy didn't wait. She jumped to her feet and kicked at his chest. He tried to grab her foot, but the blow of Amy's kick sent him against the wall. Amy jumped forward and kicked again, but this time he managed to catch her foot. He punched at her outstretched knee with his elbow. Amy screamed with pain and forced her foot down. The Masked Man used this moment to jump towards her. He punched at her face, but she was faster. She spun to one side and sent her elbow onto his throat. The Masked Man's punch missed by inches, but Amy's was right on. The Masked Man grabbed his throat, and he fell to the ground, coughing violently.

Amy staggered back, limping. She moved her weight onto her injured leg and kicked with the healthy leg at the Masked Man's head. Even though he was still coughing, he managed to block the kick. Amy fell to the ground heavily but quickly staggered up. There was a brief moment of hesitation when she was obviously wondering if she should finish the Masked Man or not. She probably thought that the Masked Man was still too dangerous for her to approach, because she limped towards the wall of the house and, using both her hands and her good leg, she climbed onto the roof.

The Masked Man pulled off the cloth that covered his face. He was coughing violently. This was Christine's chance to find out some answers. She ran around the pile of wood, quickly checking the roof. Amy was gone, and the Masked Man was breathing more calmly, coughing only sporadically. She landed on all four in front of him and looked into the face she was curious to see. The Masked Man looked up, and his eyes went round. Christine gasped and covered her mouth. They looked at each other in stunned silence.

"Hi, Christine," John said, breaking the stunned silence.

Stan, the guard who had tried to stop Amy from entering the north gate wiped his forehead with a cloth. He had been bleeding, but the cut wasn't deep, and the bleeding had stopped already. He put the cloth into his pocket and looked at the street. From around the corner, a weird guy in a suit with his hair tied in a pony tail appeared. He followed Amy, walking fast. He was sniffing the air as he walked by. The guard looked at his younger colleague who stood by the gate, watching after the stranger with his eyes nearly popping out. "You all right?" he asked him worried.

The young guard was pale and had an expression of utter shock on his face. "Stan?" he asked, not taking his eyes off the spot where the man had vanished. "That guy looked really weird. Do you think he's a werewolf?"

"Nah!" Stan said and waved his hand. There were no werewolves in the city; especially not while he was on duty. In less than an hour he would be at home and anyone could be in the city.

"Do you think we should close the gates?" the young guard asked nervously. Blood was slowly returning to his face, creating maps of red spots on his cheeks.

Stan looked at the streets and pursed his lips. He hated being the oldest guard in the group. Even though his rank was low, every other guard thought that he had all the answers. Often, he had to make decisions like this one.

"No," he said, and he shook his head. He looked at the dark gate behind him and then turned to his colleague. "There's probably no one outside that we should stop." At this precise moment, a white wolf sprinted by. He came to a halt a few yards away from the guards, sniffed the air, and bolted after Amy. Stan blinked and rubbed his eyes. He looked at his young colleague who had the same stunned expression on his face as he had before. Blood once again had left his face, leaving him even paler than before.

Stan could ignore one weird man and pretend that he wasn't a werewolf, but the wolf was harder to ignore.

"Maybe we should close the gate," the young guard said when he found his voice. It was shaking slightly.

Stan looked after the wolf and sighed. "I think you're right," he said. "Or maybe we should ask a sergeant. Closing the gate is a big decision. They should make the decision. I could go and ask—"

They heard the sound of horse's hooves from behind the gate. They both looked at each other, obviously scared.

"You're right," the young guard said. "We definitely should inform someone."

"Okay, I'll go," Stan said, and he stepped away from the gate.

The young guard grabbed his arm. "Maybe I should go," he suggested. "I can run faster to headquarters."

The sound of pounding hooves got closer. They both looked at the gate and jumped with fright as two riders rushed into the city. The riders were both pressed against their horses' necks so they could fit through the gate. They stopped abruptly in front of the guards and straightened up. Stan gasped and quickly saluted. He had been a guard in the city his whole life. In thirty years of his career, he had never met the king, though he had lived through three royal reigns—four if he counted the one who had died when Stan was a little boy. He felt as if he was in a dream, seeing the king on the horse in front of him.

"Your Majesty," the young guard breathed out, shocked. Stan wanted to kick him. He was trying to come up with a way to get the guard salute the king.

"Which way did the wolf run?" the king asked. They both immediately pointed into the street to their right. The king and the man with ginger hair spurred their horses, and both guards jumped aside to let them go through.

Oliver stood by the western gate, watching the horizon. He was bored. There were twenty more guards on and around the walls watching the same spot. They had extra duty that night because Captain Stuart expected some trouble. Oliver couldn't imagine what could have happened. Except for some weird guy coming on a horse without a saddle nearly an hour ago, nothing really had been going on. He had been a guard for a long time, and he knew not to wish for something to happen. He didn't want an eventful night; he just wanted to be in his bed at home. If he couldn't be sleeping at the moment, he'd rather be watching a boring horizon.

Suddenly, two horses appeared, approaching at a gallop. Oliver raised his hand and called out for them to slow down. When they came into the light of the torches, he saw the Royal Guards' uniforms and even recognized one of the men's faces.

Both guards stopped so abruptly that the horses' hooves made sparks as the iron rubbed against the cobblestones. "Did two people ride through here?" one of the guards barked at Oliver. "A few minutes ago?"

Oliver shook his head. "The whole evening has been very calm," he said.

"Damn!" the guard cursed and looked at the dark field behind them. "We should have split. They had to choose the north gate. Raise the alarm. Now!"

"What in the name of the gods!" Christine said, stunned. "How long— What—Why? Why didn't you tell me?"

"I'm sorry for everything," John said, and he coughed. He looked at the roof. "I will explain everything," he said, turning to face Christine. "I promise. But now I have to stop Rex from getting that stone. If Amy finds him … Go home and keep safe. Lock yourself in and close the windows because once he gets that stone, there's no telling what he'll do."

"But why? Why did you pretend to be my friend?"

"I didn't pretend," John said quietly.

"But I liked you. *Really* liked you," Christine said reproachfully.

"I will explain everything," John said. He looked around and picked up his hat. Then he looked at Christine, who watched him in disbelief. Tears were filling her eyes. She didn't understand what was happening. He leaned in and kissed her briefly and softly. Christine closed her eyes, still feeling his touch on her lips. "I promise," John whispered. Christine opened her eyes. John was already climbing the building after Amy.

"I assume this means you know the guy," a bored male voice said behind her. Christine jumped up and looked at a tall man in neat, dark clothing. His hair was tied in a ponytail. If it weren't for his pale face, he would have blended in with the shadow completely.

"Who are you?" she asked, narrowing her eyes. She was standing in a dead-end alley, and the man was blocking the only way out. He would either have to step aside, or she would have to force her way out. She was in the mood to kick someone's ass.

"My name's Bess," the man said. Christine gasped. "I think we can help each other."

"But you're a werewolf!" she exclaimed, all the courage leaving her. She wasn't afraid of a man, but a werewolf was way too strong and dangerous for her to manage. Bess shrugged and stepped closer. Christine stepped back, putting her hands in front of her protectively.

Bess stopped. "I know that I'm not welcome here," he said.

Christine stepped back some more, looking around her nervously. She could have tried to climb the building just as Amy and John had done, but she didn't believe she was capable of that. She looked at Bess, who watched her curiously. She felt so exposed there. She was like a sitting duck. Even if she screamed, no one would find her quickly enough.

"I don't mean you any harm," Bess said, sounding sincere. He lifted his hands in a peaceful manner.

Christine relaxed a little. If he wanted to harm her, he would have done so already. "What do you want?" she asked.

"I want the same thing you want."

"What would that be?"

"We both want to stop Rex from getting the stone. I think that your friend is after that very same thing. That's why he hurried away. Can you think of any place where Rex might wait for that woman?"

Christine wanted to snap back a clever retort, but nothing came to her mind. She didn't trust Bess, and she seriously doubted that he wanted to help. She opened her mouth and closed it again.

"I know that Wolfast hasn't been very friendly in the past," Bess said in an urgent whisper. Christine's eyebrow rose. "However, I was against the war. And my research suggests that Rex is very dangerous. We have to stop him from getting the stone. We need to give it to your friend once we get it, or we need to help him get it."

"Why would you want to help?"

"Because, if Norene falls, we are next," Bess said and stepped closer. Christine didn't move. "And I don't have any illusions about Wolfast. Your army is much stronger, so if Norene falls, there's no way we can hold Rex off or defeat him. Please, we're running out of time. Where do you think your friend went?"

"I must be crazy." Christine sighed. "Probably am, since until today I actually thought that the Masked Man was a stranger. Why couldn't a werewolf be willing to help?" She looked at Bess and paused. "I have no idea where they could be going," she confessed, "but I saw Rex once in the old warehouse. Maybe he's there even now. I was actually going there."

"Lead the way," Bess said, and he stepped aside so Christine could walk past him. She hesitated for a moment, but then she hurried out of the alley with Bess at her heels. As she ran through the gate, she clashed heavily into something huge and white. She collapsed to the ground, and the furry animal rolled over her. She staggered to her feet and looked at a big white wolf. The wolf jumped to its feet and looked at her.

"Hi, Daniel," Bess said in an apprehensive tone of voice. Daniel turned his head and growled at Bess, the hair on his back standing up. "I came to help," Bess added, but Daniel didn't stop growling. Horse hooves were audible in the distance, but Christine ignored them.

"What's going on?" Christine asked surprised, watching Daniel and Bess.

"I already met with Daniel here," Bess said without taking his eyes off Daniel. Daniel was growling and baring his teeth at Bess. "My kinsmen tried to kill him, but he killed them instead. You should know I was always against our coming to Norene," he added to Daniel.

Horses neighed very close, and Christine turned just in time to see them approach. She jumped aside and watched a horse stop way too close to her. She looked up, and her knees nearly gave away.

"Bess?" Ethan asked from the back of the horse. A surprised look appeared on his face. He didn't even look at Christine, whom he had nearly run over.

"Good evening, Your Majesty," Bess said, taking his eyes off Daniel.

"Ehm … Good evening?" Ethan replied hesitantly. He looked at Christine. "Are you all right?" he asked her. Christine opened her mouth, but no sound came out. She nodded vigorously. Ethan jumped down from the horse and walked over to Daniel. Daniel stepped back a little, still watching Bess. The guards from the square approached them curiously. They didn't come all the way to them, but they kept close in case Ethan wanted something.

"Why are you here?" Ethan asked Bess. He stepped between him and the growling Daniel. Daniel stopped growling and looked up at Ethan.

Bess glanced at Daniel. "I'm trying to find Rex and—"

"To help him?" Ethan jumped in. He narrowed his eyes at Bess, and Daniel growled.

"Have you ever met Rex?" Bess asked Ethan calmly, ignoring Daniel. Ethan shook his head. "I have. And I will never forget that. I didn't like the guy from the first moment I met him. I actually didn't like him even before when Mors described him to me. Even your King John knew that Rex mustn't get the stone. I will do anything to stop him."

"Anything? Even a war?" a voice said behind Christine. She spun around and looked at Lord Charles. He was sitting on a horse, leaning against the saddle. He was shooting black looks at Bess.

"I was against the war," Bess said calmly, throwing a black look at Lord Charles. "Mors was crazy and greedy. He didn't question Rex at all once Rex offered him your country. But I wanted to know who he was."

"What did you find out?" Ethan asked with curiosity in his voice.

"The worst part of the answer is here," Bess said, and he pulled a pamphlet from his pocket. "I wanted to warn you. I travelled here for that reason, but it seems that you already have the solution to this problem. I just met the man who is after Rex. So, if you can excuse me, I need to find Rex or his sidekick and stop them before it's too late."

Ethan grabbed the pamphlet and looked at it. He looked at Bess as he put the pamphlet into his belt bag. "I'm going with you," he said. "Any idea where they went?"

"This woman suspects—"

"Christine," Christine said timidly.

Bess looked at her, surprised. Then he turned to Ethan. "Christine suspects that Rex is in a warehouse in the city. I'm going to check that."

"The Masked Man is already in pursuit of that weird woman," Christine added in a high-pitched voice. Ethan looked at her, and she blushed.

"We can use Daniel's nose," Ethan said. "He can track them. He tracked them all the way here."

"Even I can smell the trail of that necklace. It's very strong," Bess said calmly. "That's how I found the woman and the Masked Man. Maybe Rex is already in the warehouse, waiting for her. The woman might want to try to get rid of the Masked Man on her way there. She might try other ways to get to the destination—longer ways. If some of us went to the warehouse, we could intercept Rex. Maybe we could split? Half of us could follow the scent, and the other half could go to the warehouse."

Ethan froze, watching Bess for a while. Then he looked down at Daniel and then over his shoulder at the guards nearby. He rubbed the bridge of his nose and with a sigh turned to Bess. "All right. Let's say that I believe you," he said. "We'll ride. We'll be faster on horseback." He turned towards Christine, who watched him, hardly breathing. "You'll ride with me," he told her. Christine blushed, not sure what to say to that. Ethan jumped onto his horse and stretched his hand towards Christine.

"All my gods!" she exclaimed, and she gingerly took his hand. Ethan pulled her up behind him. She nearly fell off the back of the horse as she sat down. She wanted to avoid touching the king, so she sat further away, but she nearly slid off the horse's rump. She grabbed Ethan's arm to pull herself up, nearly pulling Ethan after her. Ethan looked over his shoulder at her but didn't say anything. Christine mumbled an apology, her face getting hot with embarrassment. She had to use all her willpower to keep calm.

Ethan turned to Bess, who still stood by the entrance to the dead-end alley. Daniel sat in front of Bess, watching him with a mean look on his face. "You and Lord Charles follow the scent," Ethan said. "I will go with Daniel to the warehouse."

Bess nodded and stepped towards Lord Charles's horse. Daniel bared his teeth and started to growl immediately. Bess froze, eyeing Daniel with apprehension.

"He's a friend," Ethan told Daniel. Daniel stopped growling and looked up at Ethan. "I believe him. He's right. We have to stop Rex. I don't know what will happen once he gets the necklace, but I sure don't want to find out. Will you let him help us?"

Daniel stood still for a while, watching Ethan. Then he nodded. Christine had never seen a wolf nod before. It was a weird experience. Bess walked slowly over to Lord Charles's horse. Lord Charles eyed Bess with suspicion but offered him his hand. Bess took it and jumped onto the horse. The horse nervously stepped back and then to the side, as if trying to step away from Bess. Lord Charles patted the side of the horse's back, and the horse calmed down.

Daniel stood up and stepped next to Ethan. Ethan's horse neighed nervously and stepped away from Daniel. Ethan didn't pay any attention to this. He watched Lord Charles and Bess for a moment and then spurred the horse forward. Christine hadn't expected that. She yelped and grabbed Ethan's waist. On the one hand she didn't want to touch the king, on the other she didn't want to fall off the saddle. She was scared that she would fall off the horse anyway, dragging Ethan with her.

She looked over her shoulder. Daniel ran behind them, sniffing the air. Lord Charles still stood by the entrance to the alleyway, his horse nervously stepping from hoof to hoof. He was listening to Bess. Then he nodded and spurred his horse in the same direction Ethan had gone.

Christine looked in front of her. They were running by the houses of the square, approaching a smaller street to their right. Christine knew that this was a shortcut. She only hoped that it was wide enough for the horse. "Turn right," she said hurriedly when they were close to the street. "Your Majesty," she added quickly. She didn't want to sound impertinent.

Ethan nodded and turned the horse abruptly. The horse neighed and turned just in time to bolt towards a narrow street. Christine expected them to hit one side of the narrow alley as they approached the walls at such a high speed. She closed her eyes tight, holding onto Ethan's waist for her life. She heard Bess give the same instructions to Lord Charles.

Chapter 9

John was surprised at how fast Amy was. Even her hurt leg hadn't slowed her down. She was limping slightly as she ran in front of him, but he was gaining up on her. After a few turns on the rooftops, he realized that she was headed for the old warehouse. That surprised him. He thought Rex would have chosen a safer meeting point, especially when John had visited Amy there before.

Amy jumped through the gap between the houses and crashed down onto the roof of Lord Thomas's palace. She staggered to her feet and hurried along the roof, limping even more. John reached the gap and jumped too, landing on the other side without any trouble. He spotted the roof of the old warehouse in the distance.

He wondered if there was a better way of outrunning Amy now that he knew where she was headed. Suddenly, Amy stopped on the spot, spun around, and walked over to the edge of the roof. She leaned forward and looked down. Still leaning forward, she looked at John as he approached. She locked his gaze for a second, and then stepped off the roof, vanishing over the edge.

John sped up, hurrying after Amy. There was a big, dark garden at the palace with a lot of trees and shadows. If he wasn't fast enough, Amy could vanish in the darkness. He reached the place where Amy had jumped and leaned over the edge. He was expecting to see Amy running through the garden, but she was still on the ledge of the window on the fourth floor, finding her footing. John looked at the dark garden, searching for Rex. The garden seemed deserted; the whole palace seemed deserted. He held his breath and then jumped after Amy.

In his rush, he had forgotten that the facade's ornaments might not be made of stone. As he swung himself against the ornamental wooden eagle over the window, its head snapped off, and he fell heavily down onto Amy. She screamed and fell off the window ledge. Her scream was cut off as they both reached the statue above the next window, and Amy knocked off the head of a fox. John grabbed the ledge, but his fingers slipped. He hadn't even managed to slow down his fall. His hat flew away while he was trying to get hold of the ledge on the second floor. John was only vaguely aware that Amy was hitting ornaments and ledges on her way down.

Suddenly, he heard a splash below him. As he tumbled, he glimpsed Amy's dead body on the balcony as he narrowly missed it. He managed to grab the rails with his left hand. Painfully he smashed into the edge of the balcony. He bounced off towards the façade of the building, knocking off some of the ornaments. His shoulder snapped, and blinding pain shot through his arm, neck, and back. He screamed as his grip loosened and his fingers slid off the polished wood.

He closed his eyes, not sure what to expect. He landed on something and got scratches all over his face and hands as he moved closer to the ground. Then he stopped completely, his heart still racing. Hesitantly, he opened his eyes and looked around. He had fallen into a bush and had flattened it completely. By the looks of it, the bush had once been rather tall.

He heaved a sigh of relief and winced at the pain in his back and chest. He lay still for a moment, trying to process why he was still alive—and he had to be alive because death couldn't hurt this much. He realized that Amy hadn't screamed once as she fell. She had probably been knocked out when he collided with her before she landed on the balcony.

Then he remembered the necklace. She had to have it; he was sure of it. He had heard the discussion between Captain Stuart, Ethan, and the woman in the king's office. And Amy's run through the city proved that she was desperate to get somewhere. John would bet his life that it was Rex she was running to.

He staggered to his feet and out of the bush. His left arm hurt and was pretty much useless. He could move it slightly next to his body, and he could even move his fingers a little, but every movement sent a sharp pain up his shoulder. Gingerly, he palpated his shoulder, wincing at the pain. He was sure that it wasn't broken; at least he hoped it wasn't.

He looked at the bush that had saved his life. It was completely flattened. A lot of branches were broken and scattered around the pitifully looking remnant of the bush. He spun around and looked at the garden. There were way too many shadows around him. Anyone could have been hiding there. He was in no shape to search the garden at the moment. He looked up at the balcony. From down there it looked so high up. He knew he had to climb up there and retrieve the necklace, and he had to do it fast, before Rex came searching for Amy.

He walked over to the wall, his feet suddenly awfully heavy. Adrenalin was slowly leaving his body. John's back was probably totally bruised. His head hurt. He was dizzy, and every breath was painful. He wondered if he had broken a few ribs.

He pulled the cloth off his neck and used it to wipe his forehead. He didn't bother searching for his hat. He didn't need it anymore. He threw the cloth aside and grabbed the edge of a corrugation. He looked up at the edge of the balcony, wondering how to heave himself up onto it.

"Hello Pietor," a cold voice said behind John. John spun around. Rex stood by the flattened bush, his eyes aglow with green light and his lips curled in a nasty smile as he stepped towards John. "Honestly," Rex continued calmly, "I thought The League would send someone more important—or experienced."

John had no idea how Rex knew of him, but he wasn't going to show his surprise. The League knew so much about Rex, so why shouldn't Rex know about them? Especially since John had been in the city for over a month.

"Don't worry, Morgour," John replied, fighting to stand upright. "Fortis is on his way with the whole army."

"Even he's nothing compared to the power of the stone."

"Which you still don't have," John pointed out, and this time it was his turn to smile a nasty smile. "And your sidekick is dead."

"She was disposable," Rex said with a wave of his hand. "She brought me the necklace. I don't need her anymore."

"How do you know she has it?"

"You wouldn't be jumping after her if she didn't," Rex replied calmly as he stepped closer. "It was an interesting spectacle, I can tell you, but right now I'm more interested in other things. Tell me, why didn't Fortis come himself? I'm asking just out of curiosity. Why send a boy to fight his own battle?"

John was in no mood to talk. He was tired and hurting. He wished he could have taken the necklace and gotten out of there. However, if he made Rex talk long enough, he could figure out how to get to the gem, or maybe even help would come. John had never been too good with words, but now his life probably depended on whatever skill he did possess.

"He had better things to do than to deal with an outcast who wasn't strong enough even to kill him all those years ago," John snarled. It wasn't the best answer, but it still managed to wipe the grin off Rex's lips. "He claims that you were the worst of his colleagues and therefore even a novice like me could handle you," he added. Rex's eyes flashed temporarily. John stepped aside. He glanced at the balcony, trying to see some way to get up there using only one hand. He could do it if he moved beneath the edge of the balcony.

"You think that your boss is some great man," Rex hissed. John was glad that he had managed to aggravate Rex. "Don't be fooled," Rex continued, walking slowly closer. "He's just a guy who's good at using those around him. He used me centuries ago. He used everyone and everything that got in his way. He even used that fool who owned the mines in Wolfast to unsuccessfully hide the stone. It was a neat idea to hide the stone there, I admit, but he still used the people of Wolfast without even explaining them what they were guarding. And so it might be not so surprising that he used you. He would even use the stone if he knew how."

"What makes you think you can use the stone?" John asked as he stepped to his side again.

"Oh, the stone will listen to me," Rex said gleefully. "You see, Fortis knew of the stone only thanks to me. I studied the stone before I left The League. I know what it can do. I know how to use it and to what end."

"Yet it was he who figured out where the stone was," John pointed out and took another step. He was now directly beneath the edge of the balcony. A drop fell onto his cheek. He didn't need to look to know it was Amy's blood. "You probably didn't do such a great job after all," he added, wiping the blood off his cheek.

Rex's lip curved again. He sniggered and turned away from John, putting hand to his chin. "That was only a temporarily lapse," Rex said, his back turned to John.

John didn't wait any longer. He might not get such an opportunity again. He spun around and sprinted towards the wall of the palace. He jumped onto the wall and, using his healthy hand, he jumped higher up the wall, until he reached the ledge of the balcony. With his good hand, he grabbed the lower part of the rails. He tried not to make any noise as he pulled himself up onto the ledge. Once he managed to put his knee up, he knew he could do it. He pulled himself up, using his good hand for support, and then he swung himself over the top of the rails. He landed heavily onto the stone, unable to use his injured hand to stop his fall. He suppressed a groan, closing his eyes momentarily. The pain in his chest, shoulder, and back was making him lose focus. He forced himself to open his eyes. He couldn't linger. Who knew how much time he had? He looked at the garden below. Rex was nowhere to be seen.

John crawled to Amy's body, but before he could even reach her, he saw out of the corner of his eye a shadow move up the wall. In one quick movement, Rex reached the balcony and jumped in front of John.

John was about to jump to his feet when a kick landed on his hurt shoulder. He screamed and rolled over. He grabbed his shoulder, trying to block the sharp pain. Everything went blurry. He used all his willpower to make the shapes focus again. Rex was searching Amy's body. John hoped that she had lost the stone during the chase. He knew he couldn't openly fight Rex now that he was injured, but he could at least hold him off. "You can't defeat Fortis," he hissed through his teeth. The pain in his shoulder was spreading to his chest. Once again, he wondered how many ribs he had broken. He wasn't sure if he could even stand up again. He decided to try to provoke Rex—anything to make him stop looking. Rex didn't even lift his eyes off Amy's corpse. "You'll pay for everything, even if I can't stop you."

"What makes you think that Fortis can harm me?" Rex asked calmly. He looked up at John. "He didn't manage to kill me centuries ago, and he won't now."

With his unhurt hand, John fingered a dagger that was tucked into his belt. He sniggered at Rex but didn't reply. He grabbed the dagger's handle and waited for Rex to turn or at least to look down. Rex narrowed his eyes and watched John for a while. The pain in John's arm was excruciating. It got more and more difficult for him to focus.

"You can snigger all you want," Rex snapped, and his eyes flashed. John unintentionally found a weak spot. "Once I master the stone, even your fabulous Fortis will finally die. And this time I'll make sure he really does!"

John drew the dagger and threw it at Rex. The moment the dagger left his fingers, he knew it was no good. Both he and Rex watched the dagger fly through the air, bounce off the palace wall a good two feet away from Rex, and then fall down below the balcony. It vanished into the darkness with a soft clanging sound.

Rex turned to John with a nasty smile on his lips. "Nice try," he said. "Too bad you can't aim properly."

John cursed and pulled himself closer to the rails. He leaned against the cold iron and closed his eyes. He had a lot of trouble focusing on anything else but the pain. When he opened his eyes, Rex was watching him. "Don't worry. You will die soon, and the pain won't matter anymore," Rex said calmly.

"Too cowardly to kill me now?" John sniggered. He had no idea what he wanted to accomplish with this question. Maybe he hoped that Rex would stand up and walk over to him, which would give John a last chance to do something. At the same time, he had no idea what he would do.

Instead, Rex just smiled a nasty smile. "Just wait until I get the necklace," he said calmly. He resumed his search of Amy. John realized that Rex had no weapon at the moment. He had obviously been counting on finding the necklace. John reached into the pocket of his coat in search of the last ace he had. He looked at Rex and locked his gaze.

"Looking for another dagger?" Rex asked, finally pulling the necklace from beneath Amy. There was a little worry on Rex's face, which brought at least some satisfaction to John. Rex watched John intently, not even looking at the necklace in his hand. John looked at the small round gem on the golden chain. It flashed multiple times in Rex's hand. It felt to John like cry for help.

Rex looked at the stone, which was still flashing in his hand, and then grinned at John. "I bet Fortis never told you how to use this," he said. "I bet he doesn't know himself. You see, the stone has a mind of its own. It's rather funny when you think about it. It actually manipulates those people who are around it."

"It just provides answers and ideas," John said, still trying to find the object that was his last chance. Sweat erupted on his forehead.

"Answers and ideas," Rex sniggered and squeezed the golden pendant in his hand. Small fragments of gold began to fall onto the ground. "I think that's a great way to put it—answers and ideas. However, this little thing is capable of so much more," he added, and he lifted the little round stone, holding it between his thumb and a forefinger. The moonlight reflected off its shiny surface. The stone flashed once more and then remained dark. John finally located the small ring in his pocket and locked his fingers around it.

Rex looked from the stone to John, and a nasty grin spread on his face. "The best part is," he whispered, "there's no way for you to take that stone back." And with that, he swallowed it.

John watched Rex with apprehension but quickly decided that he didn't want to be anywhere near when the stone tore Rex apart or when Rex took control of it. He put the ring onto the third finger of his right hand, ignoring the sharp pain in his left shoulder as he moved the fingers of the injured hand. As soon as the inside of the ring touched his skin, he could feel energy and power inside him. He stood up quickly, jumped over the rails, and looked at the ground below. It looked way too far away for his taste. He jumped off the balcony, shooting a last glance at Rex, who was bent double, heaving hard.

John landed on the ground and rolled over to soften the fall. Thanks to the adrenalin in his body and the ring on his finger, he didn't feel any pain. He knew that the ring wasn't healing him—it was only temporarily blocking the pain—but at the moment he had more serious problem. He looked up at the balcony where Rex was leaning against the railings. John realized his mistake. He was now too far away to do anything about Rex, who was currently vulnerable. This had been John's one chance to kill the man, yet he had missed it.

Cursing under his breath, he looked around, trying to spot the dagger he had thrown at Rex. He spun around, trying to spot any glimmer or glitter of metal, but there were only shadows around him. A snigger came from the balcony. John looked up, stepping farther away. Rex was leaning against the rails, watching John. His eyes weren't shining at the moment—they actually looked completely normal—but the nasty smile on his face sent chills down John's spine.

John clutched his right hand into the fist and, kneeling down, smacked the ring against the ground. He lifted his hand off the ground and looked at Rex, whose smile froze. The ring on John's hand blinked temporarily, and eight lines of light shot out of it. They grew out of ring, followed by a thin, glass-like film. In a few seconds, a big round glass shield had formed in John's hand. He lifted himself up, his left hand hanging by his side. He put the shield in front of him, watching Rex through the glass.

On the balcony, Rex collapsed. John hoped that the stone was stronger than Rex, and that Rex would not survive it. A painfilled scream from Rex penetrated the silence of the night. John heaved a sigh of relief. The scream was cut off, and deafening silence fell. John clutched the shield tighter and stepped back. There was strong presence of magic in the air—a stiffness of the air that reminded him of the air just before a strong storm. John watched the black silhouette on the balcony, thinking hard. How much time did he have before Rex stood up? Would he manage to get up there in time?

As John jumped towards the balcony, Rex stirred and staggered onto his feet. John stopped on the spot, forming a dust cloud by his feet. He stepped back, lifting the shield in front of him. Rex straightened up and took a deep breath, spreading his hands out to his sides. He looked at the moon in the sky, ignoring John down below. John once again scanned the ground, hoping to find his dagger. He needed it right now.

Rex slowly put his hands next to his body and looked down at John. His green glowing eyes were even brighter than before. A wide grin made him look like a maniac. "Let's see how such a novice will deal with this situation," Rex said, his eyes flashing temporarily. He raised his hands and laughed as a jet of bright yellow light flashed from his fingers and flew towards John.

John closed his eyes and held onto his shield. The moment the light hit the shield, John felt only a slight pressure. He looked up surprised. Rex's laughter died in his throat. John had expected to be dead, or at least experience some difficulty with Rex's new abilities. Maybe Rex wasn't so strong after all. "Is that the best you can do?" John shrieked back at Rex. The moment he said that, he regretted it.

The look of surprise on Rex's face turned to huge grin. "For now," he whispered, and he jumped up onto the rails. "But it's not the only thing I can do," he added, standing there unmoved by the depth beneath him. He lifted his hands. A fog appeared from behind him, slowly moving in all directions. It spread away from Rex, covering him completely.

John lowered his shield a little, watching the fog over the top of the shield. He cursed. There wasn't much he could do about the fog at the moment. He needed a wide and open space to activate his defence mechanism. He had hoped that Rex would take much longer to figure out how to use the gem. Obviously, Rex had studied the stone well.

John spun around, sprinting towards the front gates of the gardens.

CHAPTER 10

E than turned left and spotted the old warehouse on the other side of
the street. Daniel ran around Ethan, sniffing the air. He looked at
the palace as he stopped. Ethan quickly pulled on the reins, and his horse
slammed all four hooves onto the ground. Christine, behind him, grabbed
his waist painfully. He didn't comment; instead, he looked down at Daniel,
who lifted his snout towards the sky. Out of the corner of his eye, Ethan
saw that Lord Charles, with Bess, had stopped right behind them, narrowly
missing them. Ethan looked over Christine's head at Bess, who was also
sniffing in the same direction as Daniel.

Bright light lightened the sky. Ethan spun around just in time to see
a fading glow above Lord Thomas's palace. His first thought was of the
people who could be in harm's way. Luckily, Lord Thomas was currently
at the castle, and his servants had a day off. They had most likely used this
opportunity to visit their families.

"I think that the necklace is there somewhere," Bess said, motioning
towards the light.

Ten guards turned the corner and stopped when they saw Ethan. They
also turned to watch fading light in the sky.

"Me, too," Ethan said with a short nod, and he spurred his horse
forward. Christine, behind him, yelped and grabbed him tighter. He
imagined that it was Joan sitting behind him on the horse, holding on
tight. For a fraction of a second, a smile appeared on his face. Then it
changed to a frown as anger kicked in again.

Lord Charles, on the horse with Bess, followed him. Daniel was next
to Ethan, matching his pace to that of the horse. Ethan stopped by the
garden gate, and the rest followed suit.

The silhouette of a man appeared in the shadows, sprinting towards the gate. Ethan couldn't see the man properly until the man reached the light from the street. The movement was familiar to Ethan, and he quickly recognized the Masked Man. The clothes matched too, though the Masked Man had lost his hat. There was a glass shield in the man's hands. Though he was sprinting towards them, he was still looking over his shoulder, only occasionally checking the road in front of him. He reached the garden gate and kicked it open. He was still looking over his shoulder as he hurried outside. Ethan wasn't sure if he should shout at him or wait to see what would happen next. The Masked Man looked at the road in front of him again and stopped on the spot, looking from Ethan to Daniel to Lord Charles and Bess.

"John!" Christine exclaimed.

Ethan looked over his shoulder at Christine, but she was already climbing down from the horse. There was worry in her voice. Ethan looked at the man in front of the garden gate. He was sure that this was the Masked Man. At the same moment, Ethan recognized the boy who had crashed into him in the opera house on the night of the ball. This meant that the Masked Man really hadn't attacked him on that one occasion. Ethan was surprised how clothes can change a man. He wouldn't have connected the boy in the opera house with the dangerous Masked Man.

John looked haggard. There were scratches on his face and hands, and his left arm was hanging loose by his body. He limped slightly. Christine hurried towards him, but John locked his gaze with Ethan's.

"Evacuate the city," he said to Ethan. His voice was normal—not the hoarse whisper he had used before. The shield in his hand blinked and then vanished.

"Does this mean that Rex got the necklace?" Bess asked, still sitting behind Lord Charles.

Christine reached John and stopped by him, checking him up and down anxiously. "What's wrong with your arm?" she asked, terrified.

John looked at Bess and then turned to Ethan. Ethan noticed that John's eyes were blue, but they lacked the mad expression his first attacker had. "Rex has the necklace," John said when Ethan didn't react. "And what's worse, he knows how to use it. He swallowed it, so we can't take it away from him without killing him. Everyone in the city is now in danger.

You need to evacuate the city. Those who choose to stay behind need to lock themselves up someplace." He turned to Christine and gently stroked her cheek. "Go to the castle," he said softly. "I can slow him down, maybe even stop him for some time, but I can't protect you in the city. Please, hurry to the castle." He turned to Ethan. "As should you, Your Majesty."

Lord Charles suddenly pointed at Lord Thomas's garden. "What's that?" he said.

They all looked in the direction Lord Charles had indicated. A fog was spreading through the garden, covering trees and statues, hiding them completely. Daniel yelped and hid behind Ethan's horse, watching the fog through the horse's legs. The horse neighed and stepped from one hoof to another.

John grabbed Christine's hand and sprinted towards the city gate, pulling her after him. Christine squealed, lifting her skirt as she ran after him. Daniel sprinted after them and vanished around the corner. Ethan could feel his skin crawl, and all his senses screamed for him to run away.

"Evacuate everyone into the castle," Ethan barked at the guards. "Avoid the fog. Inform anyone you meet." The guards saluted, and Ethan spurred his horse after John, Christine, and Daniel. Lord Charles followed Ethan immediately.

An arrow hit Ethan's horse in its right thigh. The horse neighed and kicked his back legs, jumping forward. Ethan lost contact with the saddle and felt his body falling forward. He saw the cobbles approach and quickly covered his head with his hands. He fell heavily down. He looked up, seeing the horse's hoof narrowly missing his face. He lay flat on the ground, covered his head with his hands, and waited for the weight of the horse to fall upon him any moment. The hooves hit the cobbles close to his body and then moved away from Ethan.

"Your Majesty!" someone shouted above Ethan. Ethan looked up into a guard's worried face. "Are you all right?" the guard asked and helped Ethan to his feet. Ethan looked after his horse, but it was gone already. Even Lord Charles and Bess had vanished around the corner. Ethan hoped that they had made it to the gate. Ethan stepped towards the corner, followed by the guard. Suddenly, John turned the corner, running back into the street. As soon as he spotted Ethan, he sped up.

Ethan walked towards John, glancing at the garden. The fog was seeping out of the gate, already. He looked over his shoulder at the street and stopped, surprised. There was another bank of fog spreading from around the corner. Another arrow flew out of the fog by the palace corner, hitting the guard next to Ethan. The guard gasped and fell onto the ground, staying still. Ethan looked down at him and staggered back. He looked around, searching for cover. He had never realized how wide the streets of Royal City were.

John came to a halt next to Ethan. Momentarily kneeling, he thumped the ring against the cobblestones. He lifted his hand up and stuck it in front of Ethan. The shield reappeared just in time to knock another arrow out of the air.

"Keep behind me," John shouted, jumping in front of Ethan. Ethan didn't need to be told twice. He stepped behind John, crouching. He hoped that the shield was big enough for both of them. He tried to see something in the fog, but it was too thick. John gasped, looking towards the garden. Ethan followed his gaze and saw a man at the edge of the fog. Though he was still in the fog, the fog was thin enough for Ethan to see him. The man was tall with broad shoulders. He looked unreal—too big for any human. His green glowing eyes illuminated the fog.

"So this is Rex," Ethan whispered.

"Yes," John said. He stepped back, nearly stepping on Ethan's toes. Ethan jumped back and looked over his shoulder towards the gate. The end of the street looked too far away to run. He would be hit by an arrow before he reached safety unharmed. Four guards turned the corner, running towards them, shields ready.

"Guards are coming," Ethan told John, who looked over his shoulder too.

"Keep them away from the fog," John said, and he turned back to Rex.

"What would happen?"

"The same thing that has already happened to other guards. You know … the ones that are shooting at us." The running guards reached them and lifted their shields around Ethan. "Rex is controlling them now," John continued, watching Rex apprehensively. "Everything that gets into that fog becomes a puppet in Rex's hands. Get everyone away. The fog can approach from anywhere within the city, but luckily it behaves like a real fog. If people keep within their homes with windows and doors shut, they should be safe. Those who can barricade themselves at home should do so. Those who can't or aren't sure if they can should get to the castle. I can fight the fog, but I need a bigger space for that. The fields between the city and the castle would be perfect for it. I can hold Rex off there."

"How long can you hold him?" Ethan asked, stepping back towards the gate. The guards stepped back with Ethan, awaiting orders.

"Not very long," John confessed, "but hopefully long enough for our army to get here. I sent for them three days ago, which means they should be on their way. Let's hope they get here in time."

"Can't you defeat him yourself?"

"Not now that he has the stone. He's much stronger than I am. We can try it together, but first you have to get out of here. Hurry, before more arrows come!" Ethan spun around and sprinted towards the city gate. Three guards followed him; the fourth one stayed by John.

As Ethan turned the corner, he spotted Daniel waiting for him with Lord Charles in front of the gate. As Daniel spotted Ethan, he wagged his tail and stepped forward, but Lord Charles pulled him gently back. Relief appeared on Lord Charles's face. Christine stood behind them, hands over her mouth, watching the corner with a scared expression on her face. She completely ignored Ethan. Bess was nowhere to be seen.

There were more guards by the gate, getting their shields ready. When Ethan reached them, he stopped and looked at the corner. It was very quiet there. He hated that they couldn't see what was going on. Was John all right, or had he already been consumed by the fog? What if Ethan sent guards there, and they turned the corner right into the fog?

The guards walked around Ethan, forming a defence line around him. "Keep out of the fog," Ethan shouted at them. They formed two lines in front of Ethan, and the first line knelt down holding their shields. The second line readied their bows. "Don't shoot!" Ethan quickly shouted. He hoped that the first person from around the corner would be John. It would be very unfortunate if the soldiers shot him on the spot.

Lord Charles hurried towards Ethan and stopped next to him. "I got really nervous when you didn't appear from around the corner," he told Ethan. "John said he would deal with it. He told us to stay here, and he went for you, but I got nervous, so I sent four guards after him."

"You did well," Ethan said, watching the corner. He was getting restless. He hated not being able to see what was going on around the corner. A sergeant stopped in front of Ethan and saluted. With both Lieutenant Ernest and Lieutenant Hamilton at the castle, the sergeant was in charge.

"Get as many people out of the city as possible," Ethan ordered. He quickly explained to the sergeant about the fog and possible defences. The sergeant listened intently. Ethan hoped that he understood everything.

Suddenly, John appeared, walking backwards. The fourth guard stood next to him, stepping back. The sergeant froze, watching John. "Keep that man safe," Ethan quickly said, motioning towards John, who was still walking backwards towards them. "He should be able to fight that fog once we get out of the city."

"Yes, Sire," the sergeant said, and he saluted. He hurried away and started to bark orders at the guards around them. Most of the guards moved into the city, running from door to door and checking the buildings.

John moved closer to the gate, not really paying attention to the guards behind him. When he got a few steps closer, the fog appeared from behind the corner. More arrows flew from the fog. They bounced off John's shield and landed on the cobblestones. The sergeant froze as the arrows appeared. Then he started to shout at the guards in front of Ethan. Most of the guards hurried forward to create a line of defence in front of John.

John looked around him, surprised as the guards walked past him. Before they could form the line, he shouted at them: "Get outside the city, all of you!"

The guards looked at the sergeant, who looked at Ethan. Ethan had told them to keep John safe, not to follow his orders. Since John knew best what was going on, it wasn't such a bad idea for him to give orders. Ethan nodded, and the sergeant shouted at the guards, telling them to listen to John. The guards stood up and hurried around Ethan, covering themselves with their shields. They approached the gate and left the city. Lord Charles mounted his horse again and spurred it towards the gate. Daniel hurried after him, his tail nearly brushing his belly.

Ethan decided to listen to John too. He had no idea what John's plan was, but it seemed as if he had at least some strategy in mind. Ethan turned around and, surrounded by the guards, stepped outside the city. Out of the corner of his eye, he saw that Christine was running towards the castle.

Ethan looked around the fields. Some people had already left the city through the northern gate and were running towards the castle. Guards were ushering people in through the western gate too. Most of the people hadn't noticed Ethan, but those who had slowed down to have a better look were causing more chaos at the gate. The guards were shouting at the people, encouraging them to move faster. Ethan walked farther up, looking at the fields. People were running in the distance, fleeing the city, and even more were pouring out of the gates. Ethan hoped that most people were safely in their houses with windows and doors shut, sleeping in their beds. It was lucky that it was late in the evening.

Ethan looked at the castle in the distance. The guards were helping the people into the castle. Part of the cavalry was hurrying towards Ethan. Ethan wasn't sure how much help the cavalry would be, since they couldn't cross the fog.

He looked at the gate. Most city guards were already outside the city walls. He watched the tall walls with apprehension. John had said that people could barricade themselves in houses, so Ethan assumed that the fog would be stopped by walls, city walls included. He hoped that this would be the case. The castle was a fortress that could hold off a siege for weeks, but if walls were no problem for the fog, it wouldn't matter.

The fog was creating a halo above the city walls as it approached. Ethan held his breath as he watched the tip of the white cloud move forward. It reached the walls and stopped. For a moment nothing happened, and then it moved to the sides. Ethan heaved a sigh of relief. The castle would be useful after all.

"Your Majesty!" Lord James shouted behind Ethan. Ethan spun around just in time to see Lord James stop his horse next to him. The guards on the horses continued down towards the fight.

"Create a line," Ethan shouted after the guards. "Prepare your shields. Whatever happens, don't go near the fog!"

The guards had probably heard him, because they stopped nearby and created a line right behind the guards from the city. They readied their shields, horses nervously stepping from one hoof to another. Lord James jumped down from his horse and stepped closer to Ethan, holding the reins.

"What's going on?" he asked, stunned, as he watched the people running around him.

Ethan suddenly remembered that Bess had given him a pamphlet. It probably contained some information. He opened his belt bag and pulled out the parchment. Norene had been using paper for nearly six decades now, ever since a local carpenter, Eric Peterson, had created a machine for easier preparation. Wolfast, however, still used animal skins for writing. Ethan opened the pamphlet. It seemed to be an excerpt from someone's diary. The first part was a description of a fortress. He wasn't interested in this.

A few more arrows flew from the city, and the guards readied their shields. The arrows tapped on the iron, and two men fell to the ground. Ethan looked up and then stepped farther back. He didn't need to be so close to the fighting line. Lord James followed him on foot, leading his horse by the reins.

Ethan stopped and looked at the city. People were still running out of the gates, some carrying their possessions with them. The guards were controlling the situation with a line of shields in front of the line of archers.

John stepped out of the city, hurrying away from the walls. Ethan's heart started to beat fast at the sight of him. He wasn't sure if seeing John running was a good or a bad sign. John stopped in front of the line of guards with his glass shield ready. He turned towards the city and waited for people to get out. The sergeant tried to send some guards in front of John, but he waved them away.

"What's going on, Sire?" Lord James asked again, watching the city gates.

"It's a long story," Ethan said, watching John crouch behind his glass shield. "But in a nutshell: Rex got Daniel's necklace and is now causing trouble. We need to keep John alive. It seems that his glass shield can protect us in some way. At least John said it would, though I don't know how. We need to get people to safety, and then we can lock up in the castle. I just hope that the fight will get sorted out before too many innocent people die."

"How did Rex get an army into the city?"

"That's the problem," Ethan said with a sigh. "He's using our own people. He can control anyone who gets into that fog. So it's our people against our people."

Lord James didn't say anything to this. He looked around the fields and then at the castle. Ethan looked at John, who staggered back. There was some shouting inside the city walls, and people stopped pouring outside. The guards had either redirected the rest of the people towards another gate, or it was too late, and they were now under Rex's control.

The fog appeared beneath the gate, slowly moving outside the city. John shouted something at the guards, and they all stepped back a few steps and then recreated the line. The sergeant stopped behind them, watching the fog. Ethan looked at the fields. The people were running towards the castle, but they were rather slow.

"Where are the lieutenants? And where's Lord Adrian?" Ethan asked Lord James, who was watching the city with a frown. John stepped back, making the guards rearrange the line a few feet farther up.

"They're all in the castle," Lord James answered, not taking his eyes off John. "I ordered the lieutenants to stay in the castle and prepare the defences along with Captain Stuart. Lord Adrian is overseeing the arrangements for the people from the city."

John shouted something. His shield shone momentarily, illuminating the field around him and the city walls in front of him. The shield shone again and this time stayed alight. Then the light moved from the shield in all directions, enlarging the shield. The light continued, bending a few feet above the ground and continuing towards the castle. It reminded Ethan of a huge dome. John stood by the edge of the dome, watching the illuminated gate.

Ethan looked up at the light above them. It looked like a very thin membrane that would pop any minute. It was spreading above their heads, illuminating the dark field. A bird flew towards the city, not minding the dome at all. It flew through the dome as if it was nothing and continued towards the city walls. Ethan had thought that the dome was physical, maybe made of glass, the same as John's shield, but it was just light. In the north it was spreading towards the castle, fading away far in that direction. Ethan had half expected that the dome would continue towards the ground and cover them up, but the light was losing its intensity the farther away from John it was.

Ethan looked at John, who stood still as if waiting for something. The fog crept out and started spreading in front of the gate. The guards froze and watched the fog in silence. Unnatural silence fell over the field. The fog moved away from the gate. A minute later, it reached the dome and stopped, spreading against the dome as if it were made of glass.

Ethan felt a huge relief. It really seemed that John could protect them from Rex. As the fog pushed against the dome, John staggered and stepped back. His left hand was numb by his side, his posture hunched behind the shield. A tall blob appeared in the fog, slowly moving forward. The closer to John it got, the more focused it got. When it was only ten feet away, it turned into a human silhouette. Before Ethan could see the figure in detail, a green glow spread and illuminated the fog. Rex took a few more steps until the fog was thin enough for everyone to see him clearly. He was grinning widely, his eyes aglow with green light. Ethan couldn't stare into those eyes without his own eyes watering up.

Arrows flew out of the fog and clinked against John's shield. Some missed the shield and continued through the dome towards the Royal Guards. John staggered back. His left arm was bleeding slightly. One arrow scratched his shoulder.

"Two guards—next to the man with the glass shield!" Ethan shouted. The sergeant spun around, and when he spotted Ethan, he nodded and motioned two guards forward.

"Keep the arrows from hitting him!" the sergeant shouted at the two guards who had run forward. They stopped at each side of John and lifted their shields next to John's. John didn't object. He straightened up and leaned against his shield. The fog stopped, and Rex's grin flickered.

Ethan remembered the pamphlet in his hand and quickly looked at it. He started to read it, jumping form paragraph to paragraph. Then he found the passage he was looking for:

> I found out today that the stranger was part of a very ancient organization. They call themselves The League. The man said that he needed to keep the necklace safe from a man called Morgour. It is very probable that he would use another name, but he is unmistakable because of his green glowing eyes. I have no idea what it means, but the man said that I would understand if I ever met him.
>
> If Morgour gets the necklace—

A shout made Ethan look up. More arrows flew out of the fog, but the shield was steady in John's hand. Rex stepped forward and stopped in front of the dome. John stood his ground, watching Rex apprehensively. The sergeant shouted, and the guards shot tens of arrows at Rex. Two guards with shields appeared from the fog and lifted the shields in front of Rex. They moved a little woodenly, and their faces were strangely waxy and expressionless. The arrows clanged against their shields and fell down.

The guards behind John hesitated and looked around, awaiting more orders. Rex didn't even look at the arrows on the ground. He lifted his gaze up at the dome in front of him. He tapped the dome and stepped back. Ethan breathed out. The dome was stopping Rex from crossing through. They might be able to keep him off until the people from the city got to the castle. He looked at the pamphlet and found the passage he had read last:

> If Morgour gets the necklace, he could use it right away. He would be searching for it, because it is very powerful. He would most likely use it to remove The League, with whom he had some quarrel in the past. He used to work with them, but they had a misunderstanding about the true purpose of The League. The League is trying to protect people from magic and keep balance, yet Morgour believes they should rule the world.
> The effects of the stone supposedly are—

Ethan stopped reading. He didn't need to read about the effect of the stone; he could see it in front of him. "So, world domination!" He spat the words. He looked up at the castle and saw that more archers were already on their way. Captain Stuart, on a horse, hurried after them, shouting orders at the top of his voice.

"Is that what he's after?" Lord James asked. Ethan handed him the pamphlet. Lord James took it and quickly leafed through it.

Ethan looked at Rex, wondering why Rex had had to start in Norene. Of course, he had known that the necklace was in Norene which hadn't given Rex much of a choice, but Ethan still found it unfair. Here they were, trying to fight not only for the freedom of Norene, but for the whole world. And Norene would stop him, Ethan knew. He was proud of his soldiers and his people. They would fight! And no maniac with supernatural powers would stop them now.

Lord James returned the pamphlet to Ethan and hurried down towards John. Ethan put the pamphlet away. He already had all the information he needed for the moment, and he could acquire more after they stopped Rex. Archers reached him, but they continued down towards the fight. Some soldiers stopped around Ethan, shields ready. Captain Stuart reached Ethan. "Your Majesty! You have to get out of here!" he shouted.

Ethan looked at the castle and shook his head. "I'm staying here until everyone is safely in the castle."

"Norene needs you safe and sound."

"No, Norene needs us all to stop Rex. If we fail, there won't be any Norene to rule. I'm not going to hide now."

"But if we win and you fall—"

"Then Lord Adrian will be the new king," Ethan said. "And he'll be damn good at it!" Captain Stuart opened his mouth to persuade Ethan to change his mind, but Ethan lifted his hand. "I've been hiding in the castle ever since we defeated the werewolves. I'm not hiding anymore. I will go to the castle when the last civilian is inside. Now our priority is to help John. I don't think that anyone else can do much here."

"Ready!" the sergeant shouted from behind John. Ethan and Captain Stuart looked at the sergeant. Many bows rose as arrows were aimed at Rex. "Fire!"

"Then maybe we should get to the castle and let the guards deal with it," Captain Stuart said, watching the arrows fly towards Rex. The guards by Rex's side jumped forward again, putting shields in front of him. One guard fell to the ground, but from the fog, another one jumped forward and, with the same blank expression, put his shield in front of Rex. "We should go back to the castle, especially if the fight is so uneven," Captain Stuart said as he watched Rex step over the guard's dead body towards the dome.

"We have to hold Rex off long enough for John's army to get here," Ethan said. "I'm not leaving until we succeed or perish. This isn't about my throne; this isn't even about Norene. This is about the world. And Norene will do what we do best—fight for our freedom! Fight for the freedom of the whole world!"

Captain Stuart looked around. Ethan looked around too. The guards around him were watching him. There was a murmur farther down, and Ethan would have sworn that the message was being spread like wildfire through the fields. Without a single order, the guards around Ethan turned and created two lines. The first line knelt down with shields at ready; the second one readied their bows.

Ethan looked at Captain Stuart, who was watching the guards from his horse with a strange expression on his face. Ethan had never seen that look before. It looked like pride. Captain Stuart looked from the guards nearby to the guards farther up the field. Ethan followed his gaze.

People were still walking through the gates of the city, many carrying bags and boxes. The guards were forming a line behind them to make sure that no one was harmed. Some guards were helping by carrying little children or offering their hands to the elderly people who had trouble walking. Two coaches were coming from the castle, providing transportation for those who were the slowest. The guards who were behind John were holding the shields and moving as a one man in perfect unison. The guards in front of Ethan mimicked the movement of the line behind John perfectly.

"Your presence is boosting the morale, Sire," Captain Stuart said quietly. Ethan blushed and turned his focus onto the gate.

A nasty smile appeared on Rex's lips. He lifted his hands and clapped loudly. A sound like a thunder spread through the field, and John fell down. The dome blinked and vanished. The field became dark again, illuminated only by the moonlight. The fog reflected some of the light, making it look slightly silvery. As soon as the dome vanished, the fog moved forward.

Ethan bolted down towards John. "Pull everyone back!" he shouted as he ran. Lord James looked at Ethan with a scared look on his face. This made Ethan stop on the spot. He wasn't used to seeing Lord James being scared.

John staggered to his feet with a little help from the two guards who were with him, and all three started to run towards the line of guards, narrowly escaping the fog. The guards by John's side held their shields up to cover John's retreat. A cloud of arrows flew out of the fog, covering the grassy area behind them. Another cloud of arrows from Ethan's defence line answered this attack. A few guards on Ethan's side fell to the ground. Ethan couldn't see the result of their attacks on the other side of the fog.

Lord James shouted at the guards behind John, and they started to step back as one man, making space for John. Captain Stuart spurred his horse and hurried down. The line behind John stepped back again. Captain Stuart jumped down by the defence line and staggered back. He leaned over a dead guard's body and lifted a bow from the ground and a quiver of arrows. Using the bow as a cane, he steadied himself. He reached the defence line and, with a wince, knelt at the end of the line. He lifted the bow, nocked an arrow, and aimed at the fog.

Ethan watched him for a while and then looked over his shoulder at the castle. Fear spread through him as he watched the dark silhouette of the castle. What would happen if they failed? He thought of Lord Adrian, fighting on the wrong side of the line. Then Joan's face flashed in front of his eyes, all waxy and expressionless. His knees nearly gave way. The whole world swayed for a moment.

No, they couldn't fail! That was not an option. He closed his eyes for a moment to gather his thoughts. He could hear shouts and clanging of arrows against shields. Ethan opened his eyes and looked at the fight. Captain Stuart shouted something and shot an arrow along with the other guards. Ethan watched the cloud of arrows in the air for a moment and then spun around. He hurried towards the castle and out of the range of arrows. Lord Charles stood not far away, watching the fight while standing next to his horse. He seemed a little at lost. Ethan remembered that Lord Charles hadn't been trained in battle, so the spectacle made him uneasy. Daniel sat by his side, watching Ethan intently.

Ethan stopped next to them and turned towards the gate. Daniel wagged his tail and nudged Ethan's hand. Absentmindedly, Ethan patted his head. Down by the gate, the fog continued towards them. John was running away from it, but a few feet away from the defence line, he stopped and spun around. The guards who were covering his retreat continued up, nearly tripping as they ran. They quickly noticed that John wasn't with them any longer and stopped. They both looked at John. They looked at each other and then hurried back to John, placing their shields next to him.

Ethan stared into the fog that was spreading towards them. John shouted something, and the dome spread from his shield once again, rising high up and towards the castle. The field was illuminated once again, showing hundreds of arrows sticking out of the grass. Ethan looked at the castle. The people were still running out of the city through the north gate. The rest of the gates were probably already in the fog. Ethan had no idea how many people had escaped, but he hoped that the rest were safely in their homes. And he sure hoped that the castle would be strong enough to keep the others safe. He didn't care whether he made it to the castle or not; he just hoped that his friends and the people of Norene would be safe, including Joan. The idea that they would be harmed was excruciatingly painful.

There were more shouts, and when Ethan looked down, he saw that Rex was approaching them. He was surrounded by the fog. He had a maniacal grin on his face as he watched John. His fingers looked strange in the distance. It was as if sparks were flying out of them. John stood with his feet spread wide, leaning against his glass shield. His left arm swung limp by his body. He was rather pale but seemed resolute.

Rex lifted his hands again, and another clap by Rex summoned more thunder. John didn't move a muscle. Rex's grin wavered as he clapped again. John stood his ground without the slightest hesitation. Rex's grin vanished completely. He stopped and watched John, unable to hide his disappointment. Two expressionless guards followed Rex with their shields ready.

Rex smiled nastily. At the same time as hundreds of arrows flew in the air and towards Rex, a flock of birds flew out of the fog in the direction of the arrows. The arrows and birds clashed, and most of the birds fell down dead. The guards on Ethan's side had to cover their heads with their shields as the small bodies fell down. Suddenly, another cloud of arrows flew out of the fog at a different angle, causing a few of Ethan's guards to fall down to the ground.

Ethan noticed that the birds that hadn't been hit by arrows had continued their flight towards the forest, ignoring the guards. Hopefully this meant that whoever moved *away* from the fog would become normal again. John didn't move as the birds fell. The guards by his side used their shields to keep him protected.

A strange whisper reached Ethan's ears and made his skin crawl. He looked at the forest to his right, feeling uneasy. He wasn't sure if he was imaging it, but the trees were rustling even though there wasn't any wind. The forest was whispering.

Suddenly, the dome got brighter. Ethan tore his gaze off the dark trees and looked at the fight below. The fog diminished, and lines of the Royal Guards appeared behind Rex. They all had strange expressions on their faces. They looked dead. With waxen faces and unfocused stares, they moved in complete unison. Only dead bodies on the ground were proof that the standing people were still alive.

Ethan wondered what Rex really wanted. There were many forms of world domination. Was it the throne, slaves, weapons, land? Ethan was in no mood to ask Rex, but it was a little unnerving not to know the worst-case scenario. Somehow, death didn't look so bad in comparison to those empty faces of his own people.

Ethan's imagination immediately offered him an image of Rex standing on a battlefield with an army of Ethan's people behind him—Lord Adrian with a vacant expression shooting an arrow and being shot down like something expendable. Ethan closed his eyes and shook his head.

Rex stopped by the dome and looked around. Another volley of hundreds of arrows flew towards Rex, and another flock of birds stopped it. This time the guards were ready for the additional arrows and managed to stop the attack without any losses. The forest whispered once again, much louder this time. Ethan's skin crawled, but he couldn't see anything unusual when he glanced at the trees. Something was happening in the forest, but since he had no idea what, he decided to deal with the direct threat in front of him.

Ethan knew that Rex had to run out of people and birds—and arrows—at some point. And Ethan's army had plenty of arrows and only one target. This was a huge disadvantage for Rex. Most of the city guards had only swords, which were useless to him now. All those who got into the fog became his puppets. If he sent anyone out of the fog, he would lose control. It wasn't so bad after all.

As soon as this thought occurred to Ethan, sparks flew out of Rex's fingers. He looked down, and a satisfied expression crossed his face. Chills ran down Ethan's spine. Suddenly, a flash of golden light shot out of Rex's fingers. It hit John's glass shield with a thud. John collapsed, hardly able to keep the shield up. The guards by his side tried to pull him up, but John remained kneeling behind the shield. Ethan's smile vanished. Apparently mind-controlling fog and heavy thunder weren't the only weapons Rex had.

John staggered to his feet. He held the shield in front of him, but it seemed as if he was losing the energy he needed to fight. They all stepped back—John with the two guards and the two lines of guards behind them. Rex smiled nastily and sent out another jet of light. This time John expected it and stood his ground, but the pressure moved him farther away, digging his feet into the ground.

Bess reached the forest by the castle and sprinted in among the trees. He stopped and looked around. A crowd of people was running towards the castle. They consisted of old and young, women and men, poor and rich. Their retreat to the safety of the castle was covered by the Royal Guards. Another big group was down by the city, fighting off Rex's men. The rest stayed in the castle, organizing the situation.

Lord Charles stood with the king between the castle and the fight below. As Bess watched them, Lord Charles said something to Ethan and then jumped onto his horse and spurred it towards Lord James. Daniel moved forward, but Ethan placed his hand on Daniel's back, and Daniel sat down, watching Lord Charles hurry towards the guards below.

Captain Stuart retreated to the second line of defence and then moved farther up north, leaning against the bow in his hand. He continued giving orders to the guards who were helping people to the safety of the castle. His voice was getting hoarse from all the shouting. Bess watched Captain Stuart curiously. He hadn't seen the captain since the night he had left the castle and was surprised at how bad the captain looked. He was much slimmer and had lost most of his muscle tone. He was limping, his hand was bandaged heavily, and he was rather pale.

Bess looked down at Rex, whose eyes were aglow as he sent one lightning flash after another at John. John was still slowly retreating, covering behind his shield. Lord James was standing by the lines behind John, occasionally sending arrows at Rex, who smashed them to pieces with the lighting. All his energy seemed to be focused on John only. The Royal Guards were backing away. Rex was slowly but surely moving forward. He would soon reach the castle. And once he had finished with Norene, he would turn his focus southward. Wolfast was next. Wolfast now needed Norene to succeed more than ever.

Bess turned to the forest and looked at the dark trees. He wasn't sure if he could be of any help or not. No one had noticed when he had left because no one had missed him in the fight. Since he had no bow and arrows and no right to order Ethan's army, he knew he was of no use to them—in a conventional way. There was another possibility, and Bess was curious to try it. The forest felt very restless. Bess could feel the tension in the air. Hopefully he wasn't wrong. He threw his head back and howled like a wolf.

CHAPTER 11

Ethan looked at the forest, surprised. Daniel peeked around Ethan's knees and looked at the forest, tilting his head to left. Ethan had never heard a wolf cry like that. It sounded like a monster's cry. That had to be what a werewolf sounded like. Had Rex managed to get Bess under his control? Ethan hoped to see more of the forest, but it was way too far away from John and from the light of dome. Only now he realized how bright the light of the dome was.

Ethan tore his eyes off the forest and looked at the fight below. John was having a lot of trouble keeping Rex at bay. Most of the people were already in the castle. Those who hadn't managed to get out of the city were either safely in their houses or fighting against their will by Rex's side.

Another bolt of lightning flew against the barrier, and John knelt down. The fog moved forward faster even though the dome created by the shield hadn't diminished. John staggered to his feet and shouted something at the guards behind him. He was leaning against his shield, but the fog was pushing it back. The defence line stepped back, and then, on Lord James's order, turned around and sprinted towards the castle. Lord James stayed behind with ten guards who wielded shields. The two guards by John's side looked over their shoulders but stayed put. Ethan spun around too and hurried away. He looked over his shoulder and saw that John was walking backwards, holding the shield, the two guards by his side.

Ethan turned around, running towards the castle. He was halfway up with Daniel at his heels when Daniel stopped and yelped. A wave of fear washed over Ethan. He spun around, half expecting to see Daniel dead on the ground, but Daniel wasn't hurt. There was no arrow sticking out of Daniel's body, and he wasn't even lying on the ground. He wasn't even watching the battle below. He stood like a statue, watching the woods, the hair on his back completely rigid and upright. Ethan followed his gaze and looked at the dark forest.

Flashes from Rex's attack lit trees at the edge of the forest. Ethan frowned. He wasn't sure if it was the play of the light, but he thought he saw a shadow moving in the forest. With every flash, the forest looked a little different. Ethan looked down towards the fight. John was still standing, slowly stepping back. The fog was moving forward, pushing at the shield. Rex's flashes of lightning were constantly attacking John, occasionally sending him to the ground. The guards were hurrying to the castle. This was an organized retreat. Lord Charles stopped close to Lord James. They had a quick discussion. Then Lord Charles hurried back, reaching the retreat line, while Lord James hid behind a tall shield as he stepped towards John and the two guards.

Ethan looked at the forest again. The trees vanished in a huge shadow. It was like looking at a completely different world. The forest was so dark that Ethan couldn't make out anything, not even the trees on the edge. Then the shadow moved a bit more, and Ethan realized that the shadow was a group of animals running out of the forest. There were deer, bears, wolves, foxes, birds, even bunnies. Ethan couldn't make out all the animals in the dark mass. There had to be hundreds of them. They all sprinted towards John and the guards. And Ethan was in their way.

Another flash illuminated the animals. Ethan's heart started to beat painfully in his chest as the animals became dark again. His head spun, and his breathing quickened. Then the realization dawned on Ethan. He was now looking death in the eye. This was it. His heartbeat slowed down rapidly, and his head cleared. He took a deep breath and stood up straight.

He had hoped he would reign longer than a few months, but sometimes these things couldn't be helped. He was not going to die a coward. He could not stop all the animals, but he could fight. He drew his sword and turned to face the racing darkness in front of him. He lifted his sword above his head, tightening the grip on the hilt. The animals approached him from the west, the guards were running from the south, escaping the fog, and the last of the people who had managed to escape from the city were running towards the castle in north. In a few minutes the people would be safely in the castle where Lord Adrian would take care of them.

Ethan's job was finished for now. He had one last task to do, and since the guards were too far away, he had to do it alone.

Daniel walked around Ethan and stepped in front of him. Ethan had completely forgotten about Daniel. He wanted to shout at him to run away, but the words died in his throat as another bolt of lightning illuminated the mass in front of them. Daniel sat down with his back turned to Ethan. Then he tilted his head to the left. Ethan smiled. Daniel reminded him of a puppy. He was obviously curious about the danger in front of him, and obviously did not fully realize the situation they were in. At least Daniel would survive this. He might need a few days to heal, but he would be all right. This was very calming thought for Ethan.

The animals were a few jumps away. Ethan got ready and raised his sword. He planned to smite the first animal that approached him. Suddenly, the mass of animals parted and sprinted around Ethan and Daniel. Daniel curiously looked around as another flash of light illuminated the field. Ethan stood rigid for a while and then turned around, lowering his sword. The animals were running towards the guards, but they avoided collision as best as they could. A few surprised guards didn't have any chance to jump aside, but most understood very quickly that the animals were not after them. The retreat was stopped, and the guards created paths through their ranks for the animals.

Ethan looked up again and spotted a bear with a human silhouette riding on his back. He readied his sword again and waited for the apparition to get closer. Daniel looked up at Ethan and then turned towards the bear. He growled, all the hair on his back standing up. The bear slowed down and walked towards them nonchalantly while the rest of the animals ran around them and towards the fight below. Another flash of light illuminated the man on the bear. Ethan heaved a sigh of relief. "How the hell did you do that?" he asked, lowering his sword and motioning towards the animals around them.

"I studied," Bess answered and jumped down from the bear. The bear immediately ran around them and joined other animals. "It's surprising how little the werewolves know about their own abilities." Daniel growled some more. Bess stopped abruptly and looked at him. Ethan stepped to Daniel and patted him on the head. It was an automatic reaction, but it worked. Daniel looked at Ethan surprised and stepped back.

"What happened?" Ethan asked, motioning at the animals around them. There were hundreds of them. Ethan wondered if they all lived in the forest or if they had come from farther away. The last of the deer ran around them and sprinted down towards the fog.

"I asked them for help," Bess said calmly, watching the animals.

Ethan turned around and looked down. "So you made that howl?" Ethan asked. Bess nodded. "That was an awful sound, you know," Ethan added, watching the fight.

"I know," Bess said quietly. "I used to be a human in werewolf country. I heard them howl like that a lot. When you don't know what it means, it's rather scary, especially when you're alone on a street during the night."

"Why in the name of the gods would you be in the middle of the night outside in a country full of werewolves? That's suicide!"

"Tell me about it."

"Tell them to stop where they are!" Ethan said quickly, suddenly seeing danger for the animals—and for them. It was obvious that the animals were sprinting into the fog. "If they hit the fog, they become Rex's puppets."

"I know that Rex is controlling everyone, but I can't control the animals. I only asked them for help. All those dead birds Rex used as a shield enraged the animals, and they decided to act. I can't stop them. I can't order them either. And I can't explain to them the danger of the fog. Maybe Daniel here can communicate with them more easily than I can." As a response, Daniel growled at Bess. "Or not," Bess added calmly.

Ethan stepped forward and watched the fog with dread. Hundreds of animals sprinted down towards the city, avoiding John and the guards the same way they had avoided Ethan and Daniel. Ethan expected them to stop when they hit the fog and turn around, but the momentum of their running steps was so strong that they were like rolling stones. Even Rex couldn't stop them. He managed to avoid collision by jumping aside. Unlike the guards, the animals didn't know they should aim at Rex. They knocked most of the guards behind Rex out of the way. Then the fog moved back.

"It's working!" Ethan shouted, and he slapped Bess's back. He hadn't believed that anything could stop Rex's approach. Rex screamed with rage and stepped back a few steps avoiding more animals. John straightened up. This was the first time that the fog wasn't diminishing the effect of his shield.

Christine sprinted up the drawbridge. Lord Adrian was standing by the gate, shouting at people and guards alike. Captain Stuart was limping with the line of guards towards the castle, watching the fight below. Though the fight was too far away for any arrow to reach them, Christine was grateful for this safety line. She pushed her way through the gate and looked around. She had lived in Royal City her whole life, but this was the first time she had actually visited Royal Castle. She'd seen it once when she was a little girl from afar, but only now did she reach those tall walls.

She stopped and looked in awe at the magnificent building in front of her. The castle was carved into the mountain, which was taller than the tallest tower. Christine breathed out and then looked at the walls. The guards were on the walls, watching the fight in the distance. Christine looked at the castle. There was a long balcony on the second floor. She couldn't go to the walls—the guards wouldn't let her—but she could watch it all from the balcony.

She turned on the spot and nearly crashed into Lord Adrian, who was organizing the refugees. He completely ignored her as she mumbled an apology and then hurried through the yard towards the castle. The people were pouring into the castle, looking lost. The Royal Guards were directing them to the underground system of tunnels where they would be safe from harm during the fight.

Christine ran through the yard and climbed the stairs, taking two at a time. She had to stop at the top of the second floor to catch her breath, but otherwise she didn't linger. No one was paying her any attention as she hurried down the corridor. It didn't take her too long to find the balcony. She stepped out, watching the fields in the distance. The fight looked awful from up there. Lights in the distance looked like flashes of lightning. Christine wasn't sure if she was imagining it. It was difficult to distinguish details in the darkness, but it seemed as if animals were running towards the heart of the fight.

A quiet sob made her look to her right. A young woman stood by the railings, watching the fight. Christine recognized her from the ball. It was Lady Joan. She hadn't acknowledged Christine's presence. Tears were running down her cheeks as she watched the fight.

Christine didn't care. There was only one thing that mattered to her at that moment. She looked at the fields, searching for John.

"You should get out of here," Bess said to Ethan, and he motioned towards the castle. Ethan looked at the dark silhouette of the castle behind him. It was repeatedly being illuminated by flashes of lightning.

"We need to get John into the castle," Ethan said. "If he falls, it won't matter where I am."

They both looked at the fight below. Rex kept on hitting John's shield repeatedly with flashes of lightning. He had a maniacal grin on his face, his green eyes shining brightly. There were bodies of dead animals all around him, but some had survived the collision and were now alongside others who were Rex's puppets. The fog was getting thicker, slowly hiding more and more of Rex's army. John was standing upright again, holding his shield.

The Royal Guards still sent arrows repeatedly to cover their retreat, but the flashes of lightning were stopping all the arrows with ease. The guards under Rex's influence occasionally sent arrows through the fog.

A cloud of arrows flew through the air and landed against the shields around John. The guard to John's right fell to the ground and stayed down. Ethan stopped breathing, expecting an end, but Lord James immediately detached from the ranks of the last guards and jumped to John. He put his shield above John and grabbed the fallen man's shield. He lifted it in front of himself, steadying himself against John's shoulder. Lord Charles spurred his horse, hurrying towards the castle.

Another group of arrows flew through the dome at Rex and his puppets. The lightning smashed them to pieces, though a few fell through. The arrows landed amongst Rex's puppets or clanked against the shields. The Royal Guards shot a second group of arrows. The guards on Ethan's side were trying to avoid killing the guards on the other side if they could.

They were mainly aiming to stop the enemy's advance. Ethan understood why. Those people weren't acting of their own accord. They were friends and family members of those on the other side of the fog. But those guards under Rex's influence weren't so friendly. Rex's orders were simpler: kill as many as you can. The worst part was that the pain wasn't stopping the puppets. They were like zombies or wooden dummies. They ignored the arrows sticking out of their legs or arms. They attacked until they ran out of arrows. Then they pulled the arrows out of their flesh with vacant expressions and shot them back at John and the guards. Only death could stop these puppets.

John, along with Lord James and the other guard, moved farther away from the fog, stepping towards the safety of the castle. Ethan looked over his shoulder at the castle. All the people who had run from the city were already inside. Even Ethan wasn't that far away now. With horses, they could get to safety fast enough.

"Look out!" Bess shouted. Ethan spun around. Before he could see anything, he was thrown to the ground. Bess fell on top of him heavily. Ethan rolled Bess off and looked around. The retreating guards moved closer, keeping their backs to Ethan and the castle. Ethan didn't understand what was going on.

Then he spotted many arrows sticking in the ground around him. Bess groaned, lying on the ground, face down. Ethan rolled him over. A broken arrow protruded from his chest. Ethan looked at the arrow in disbelief. His mouth had gone completely dry, and his mind was empty. He needed Bess to survive the fight. Bess was the only normal werewolf Wolfast had ever known. He was actually trying to make peace with Norene. What if they survived Rex's attack and then had to deal with a new leader in Wolfast?

He grabbed the shattered wooden shaft and pulled the arrow out of Bess's chest. Bess screamed. Ethan ignored Bess's protest as he quickly, with his hand shaking, cleaned the tip of the arrow against his trousers. He looked at the cleaned tip, trying to figure out what it was made of. Another lightning bolt hit the dome, and the tip was illuminated. Ethan heaved a sigh of relief and threw the arrow to the ground. The tip was iron. "Why in the name of all the gods did you do that?" he asked Bess as he pressed his hand against the bleeding wound.

"I will survive this," Bess said in whisper to Ethan with a grin on his face. He was paler than normal. A grimace of pain twisted is face for a moment. "You wouldn't," Bess added.

Ethan shouted at the nearest guards. They looked around and, when they spotted Ethan, they jumped to him. Three used their shields as a roof over Ethan and Bess; the other two jumped to Ethan. "Take him inside," Ethan ordered and motioned to Bess. "Hurry!"

The guards picked Bess up from the ground and carried him, half running, half staggering, towards the castle gates. Ethan watched them for a moment and then turned towards the fight. Lord Charles reached him and stopped his horse nearby. The guards behind John were still retreating. Ethan and Charles, who was still on horseback, were close now, watching the fight below. John and Lord James were also stepping back. It seemed that John was standing on his feet only thanks to Lord James and the guard to his left. The guards around Ethan, protecting him with their shields, waited for Ethan's orders. Ethan watched John and Lord James, absentmindedly wiping his bloodied hands on his shirt.

They had to get John into the castle. There they could figure out what to do next. Would they be able to outrun the fog? It was sure that they had to try. Ethan jumped to his feet and walked around the guards to Lord Charles. "Give me your horse!" Ethan shouted at him. Lord Charles tore his gaze off the fight below and looked down, surprised. His gaze fell on Ethan, and he nodded. He unhooked his right foot from the stirrup and was about to swing his leg over the saddle when a huge lightning bolt made the fields so bright that Ethan had to cover his eyes. Lord Charles's horse neighed. A heavy blow hit the shield, and the ground shook beneath Ethan's feet. The light diminished, and Ethan blinked into the darkness. The dome was still shining, but compared to the bright light of the lightning, it was way too dark. The guards around Ethan and Lord Charles came to focus. They were watching the shield with dread.

Lord Charles's horse stood up on the hind legs. Ethan jumped back, avoiding the hooves and watched Lord Charles grabbing the saddle frantically. Another blow hit the shield, and the horse lost its footing. It tilted further and threw Lord Charles from the saddle. Lord Charles fell heavily onto the ground with a grunt. The horse neighed as it tilted more and started to collapse onto Lord Charles. Ethan shouted and jumped forwards, but he was too slow to pull Lord Charles away. Lord Charles screamed and covered his face.

Out of nowhere, Daniel appeared and jumped at the horse. His wolf form looked so small in comparison with the huge horse, but he managed to push it aside. The horse narrowly missed Lord Charles as it crashed to the ground. Daniel fell down onto the ground and rolled all the way towards the dome. Ethan screamed at top of his lungs, but nothing could be done to stop Daniel's movement. He continued to roll until he landed on the other side of the shield, surrounded by the fog.

Ethan completely forgot about Lord Charles on the ground. He completely forgot about the guards with shields held as a roof over his head. He forgot about John and Lord James, who were trying to get back to the castle. He completely forgot about Rex and his constant attacks on the shield and the dome that was protecting them. The sounds around him diminished, and the constant flashes of lightning faded. The only thing Ethan could think of at the moment was Daniel. Now Rex had Daniel on his side. It felt as if they were losing their advantages. Daniel was under Rex's influence, and Bess was wounded in the castle. Even John was getting weaker with every moment.

Lord Charles staggered to his feet and looked around. At first, he looked startled, but then Ethan realized that Lord Charles could try to pull Daniel back. Ethan jumped towards him. Lord Charles looked at Daniel's limp body and moved forward. Ethan grabbed Lord Charles's shoulder to stop him from approaching the dome.

"We can pull him back!" Lord Charles said as Ethan pulled him farther from the dome. "He's not that far away," he added and pointed at Daniel's limb body.

"Maybe even the smallest touch of the fog could turn you into Rex's puppet," Ethan pointed out. Lord Charles stopped fighting him. "We have to stop Rex. Once he's dead, those people will be free, including Daniel. Don't walk to the other side. You won't help anyone."

Daniel lifted his head and looked in front of him. A breeze was playing with his fur as he lay still, looking at Rex. Gingerly, he stood up and shook himself. Then he stepped towards Rex, hardly looking left or right. Ethan noticed that his step was different from others on that side of the fog. While the others looked like puppets on strings, their movements jerky,

Daniel's movement was fluent and resolute. There was some purpose in his step. There was something there that gave Ethan hope.

Daniel walked closer to Rex, avoiding the dome. He kept in the fog, but the fog was thin enough on the edge for Ethan and Lord Charles to see Daniel. They watched him with their mouths gaping open. Ethan hadn't even noticed that he was still holding Lord Charles's shoulder.

Daniel reached the line between Rex's puppets and Ethan's Royal Guards. Then his pace quickened. A few steps later, he started to trot, and then he broke into a run. Ethan let go of Lord Charles and stepped closer, watching Daniel running towards Rex. There was no doubt about it now; Daniel could enter the fog without being affected by it.

Rex's total focus was on John. John was leaning against Lord James, holding onto the glass shield. Rex sent another bolt of lightning, and the shield in John's hands cracked. The dome blinked and vanished, throwing them into temporary darkness. Rex's eyes were so aglow that his face was completely illuminated. A nasty grin appeared on his face as he sent a strong bolt of lightning towards John. The shield in John's hands cracked some more, and John staggered. Rex laughed loudly and sent another bolt. The earth shook beneath Ethan's feet. John, Lord James, and the guard flew a few yards into the air. They all fell heavily onto the ground. John's shield shattered completely, and the fog bolted forward.

Daniel still sprinted along the ranks of Rex's puppets. John staggered to his feet and collapsed again, staying down. The remnants of the shield lay all around him. Lord James remained on the ground, his body twisted in an unnatural position. The second guard crawled away from the advancing fog, collapsing soon afterwards.

Rex laughed again and stepped forward. The laughter sent chills down Ethan's spine. His throat had gone completely dry as he watched them. Daniel reached Rex and jumped onto him. At the last moment, Rex looked at Daniel. Laughter died in his throat. A shocked expression replaced the grin. He didn't put his hands in front of his face; he didn't even scream. He just watched Daniel's teeth, his green eyes wide.

Daniel's paws landed on Rex's shoulders and pushed him backwards towards the ground. His teeth, without slightest hesitation, found Rex's throat and dug deep. Suddenly, every sound stopped. Ethan felt as if he had gone completely deaf. A bright light illuminated the fields, spreading in all directions. Then it blew up without causing any sound. It was a strange spectacle as the ball of light bolted forward. It created so much light that Ethan couldn't look at it. He closed his eyes and turned his face away. And then the blast came, nearly tearing Ethan's eardrums. A strong wave of energy followed, throwing everyone in its way to the ground.

The light reached the castle, banging heavily against the walls. The castle shook. Then the light moved forward, throwing everyone, including Christine and Joan, off their feet. Christine landed on the hard stone of the balcony. Then the sound of the blast came, deafening Christine temporarily. Then everything went quiet.

Christine gulped and gingerly sat up. The castle was dark. If it weren't for the moon in the sky, she wouldn't have been able to see anything. She staggered to her feet and, using the rails of the balcony, she pulled herself up. She stared at the fields, but there was darkness everywhere. Even torches inside the castle had been blown out. A strong pressure grabbed her heart, and her voice froze in her throat. She feared that this meant that John was dead.

CHAPTER 12

Ethan groaned and lifted his face from the ground. He looked up. He was lying on his belly on the pitch-black field. His ears were ringing loudly, suppressing any sound around him. Then the moon appeared from behind the cloud. Though it wasn't a full moon, it cast enough light so that Ethan could see more than just silhouettes.

The guards were staggering to their feet, looking around, surprised. John lay still farther away. Ethan wondered if he had survived the weird phenomena, but then John moved his right hand beneath himself and slightly lifted his head up. He looked straight ahead for a moment and then put his head back down. Ethan followed his gaze.

Rex lay on his back with the blank expression on his face turned towards the sky. Ethan couldn't see him properly, but he recognized a dead body when he saw one. Next to him lay Daniel, on his side. The breeze was slightly moving his fur, but that was the only movement. Ethan lifted himself up onto his knees and touched his head. It hurt like hell. He felt something wet. He looked at his hand and saw something dark on his fingers. Great! He was bleeding! Again!

He looked at the castle over his shoulder and felt relieved when he saw it standing there. Torches were being relit, and the castle was becoming brighter with every second. Ethan's head hurt and his ears were still ringing, but it was all nothing compared to strange pain in his chest. He looked at Daniel's body again, and a stab went through his heart.

Lord Charles stirred next to Ethan and looked up. Their eyes met, and Ethan wordlessly nodded towards Daniel. Lord Charles followed his gaze. "Oh, no," he mouthed. Ethan wasn't sure if Lord Charles produced any sound because all Ethan could hear was ringing in his ears.

Lord Charles staggered to his feet and hurried to Daniel. Ethan stood up too and followed him, feeling dizzy. It took them a while, but finally they reached Daniel's body. Lord Charles fell down on his knees next to it, shaking it. Nothing happened. Ethan reached him and collapsed nearby. His head turned and ached.

Lord Charles lifted Daniel's lifeless body and shook it some more. Ethan reached out and grabbed Lord Charles's shoulder. "He'll wake up," he whispered. "It's very difficult to kill Daniel, you know," he added. He wasn't sure if Lord Charles could actually hear him. Lord Charles carefully put Daniel's body down and put his head into his hands.

As a breeze blew over them, Daniel's body was covered by a cloud of dust. Then Ethan realized that the cloud was forming a shape. It was a human body. Lord Charles lifted his head and watched the apparition with his mouth gaping open. The cloud grew bigger until it took shape of Daniel's ghostly human form. A slight glow radiated out of the shape, illuminating everything around him, including Daniel's lifeless body on the ground.

Daniel's ghost looked around, and then he spotted Ethan and Lord Charles at his feet. He crouched down, temporarily getting out of focus. The dust was still for a moment. For a little while, Daniel became a formless cloud, and when he came into in focus again, a wolf was standing in front of Lord Charles.

Daniel's ghost leaned in towards Lord Charles, who watched him with tears in his eyes. Daniel stepped closer and rested his head against Lord Charles's chest. Lord Charles gasped. Then he gingerly lifted his fingers and touched Daniel's ghostly form. The fur moved under his touch. Lord Charles hugged Daniel, and they stood still for a moment, Lord Charles shaking slightly. Ethan blinked away the tears. Then Daniel stepped back. Lord Charles put his head into his hands while Daniel turned to Ethan. It was strange to look into Daniel's face now. It was like trying to see a shape in a fog. Whenever Daniel moved, the image blurred, and Ethan had to blink to refocus again.

Daniel stepped towards Ethan and tilted his head to left. Ethan smiled and reached out, trying to pat Daniel's head. Daniel stood still as Ethan's hand touched him. It felt strange. It was as if Daniel was solid and at the same time made out of fog. Ethan's hand felt a pressure, yet his eyes tried to convince him that he was touching a thin air.

Daniel nudged Ethan's face, leaving a cold feeling on Ethan's cheek. Then the shape of Daniel became blurry again, but this time it didn't reform into a visible shape. A few moments later, the breeze scattered the remnants of the dust in front of Ethan.

Ethan met Lord Charles's gaze. Tears were running down Lord Charles's cheeks. "He came to say goodbye," Ethan whispered. Through the ringing in his voice he couldn't hear his own words. "He's not ever going to wake up," he added. Lord Charles picked up Daniel's body and hugged it in his arms, shaking as he buried his face in Daniel's fur.

Ethan blinked away tears and staggered to his feet. He had to find something else to do to release the pain in his chest. He looked around. Most of the guards around them were watching them, but some were approaching John and Lord James. The guards and the people on the other side of the fog looked around. They seemed puzzled. The fog was slowly lifting, and so was the spell over them. The animals looked around. They also seemed momentarily surprised. It was a strange spectacle—people and animals side by side, looking at each other stunned. Then the animals bolted towards the forest, slaloming between the people. The fog's power was gone.

A guard knelt down next to John, said something, and then stood up, turning to Lord James. Most of the guards were gathering around Lord James. Ethan sighed and walked over to them. The guards stepped aside to let Ethan through. Ethan stopped at the edge and looked down at Lord James's body. The guards had turned him onto his back and neatly placed a sword in his hands. Ethan looked at the calm expression on Lord James's face. He looked as if he was sleeping, but there was something missing in his expression.

Ethan stepped forward, knelt by his body, and placed his palm on Lord James's forehead as tradition dictated. He closed his eyes and lowered his head. The pressure in his chest tightened. "Thank you for everything," he said to Lord James's body, his voice shaking. Then he stood up. He looked around at the gathered guards. He took a deep breath and then raised his voice: "A great warrior left us with the best gift he could have bestowed upon us: his life for ours. He will live in our memories and hearts, and history will remember him as the hero he was."

Ethan didn't know if the guards heard him. The ringing in his ears was diminishing, and he could once again distinguish other sounds. The guards around knelt down. They placed their right hands on their chests and bowed their heads to Lord James. The guards behind the first line mimicked them. The wave of kneeling guards moved towards the castle. On the walls, the guards did the same, and Ethan could see in his mind's eye that so did the guards inside the castle. They might not know who had fallen, but they knew that it was an officer. It was someone who would be missed by everyone. Ethan looked towards the city. Citizens and guards who were under the spell were still confused, though a few knelt.

Ethan lowered his head and stepped back, leaving space for the shield that had been sent from the castle. A few guards stepped forward and carefully lifted Lord James's body onto the shield. They lifted it and carried Lord James's body towards the castle. Then the guards, one by one, stood up, turned, and walked behind Lord James.

Ethan watched after them until they vanished inside the castle walls. The torches were being distributed from the castle to light the fields properly, and the guards were cleaning up the place. He blinked and wiped a tear off his cheek. He turned towards John and knelt down. "You need a doctor," he told him.

Luckily, the ringing was fading; otherwise, he wouldn't have been able to hear John's voice, which was muffled by the dirt. "I'm fine," John whispered, and he lifted himself onto his right elbow. He looked forward towards Daniel's and Rex's bodies. "Is Rex dead?" he asked.

Ethan looked at Rex's lifeless body. The guards were first looking after those who had survived, but had been hurt. They would take care of their own fallen fellows when everyone was safe. So the body of Rex was left forgotten at the moment. Lord Charles still knelt by Daniel's body, his head in his hands. Ethan wanted to comfort him but didn't know how. He quickly turned his focus on John. "Do we need to make sure he stays dead?" he asked.

John laughed. "Honestly, I don't know," he said. "Beheading should be a safe way."

Ethan wasn't one who would mutilate a corpse, but since he had met the werewolves, he had changed. He wasn't against this plan. And this was a special circumstance. "We'll deal with the body," he said shortly as he straightened up. "Now, let's get you into the castle," he added and helped John to his feet. John staggered up and leaned on Ethan. Ethan immediately felt that John was shaking. Ethan prodded John and turned towards the castle.

"I think I can walk," John said feebly, unsuccessfully trying to stand up straight. He winced, and his knees gave way. His entire weight fell onto Ethan, who managed to keep John from falling.

"I'm sure you can," Ethan said calmly, and he pulled John to his feet again. John leaned against Ethan.

"You're the king," John pointed out. "You have people who are meant to help others."

"You're a hero," Ethan replied, and he slowly stepped towards the castle, supporting John. "And there are plenty of people around who need help. I can put my hand in on this one."

They continued up the hill towards the castle. Ethan had always known that the castle was slightly uphill from the city, but only now did he truly feel the ascent. They walked in silence for a moment, but Ethan's curiosity was too big. He had so many questions he wanted to ask. But where to start? "Who are you?" he asked.

John looked at Ethan and smiled. "It's a difficult question to answer," he said. "But I'll try to answer it. At least those parts I know … I don't know how long ago it was, and I don't even know how it started, but a group of creatures was created from all over Lanland. These were people with special abilities. Some, like me, were humans, but some were much stronger magical beings like Rex. I joined four years ago after I tried to escape a group of attackers in Welhair country. I escaped across the roofs of the city and managed to leave the country."

"Welhair?" Ethan asked, frowning. "I've heard of that place. It's like a fortress somewhere in the south of Lanland. They say that it's impossible to get there."

"Yes." John nodded. "That sounds about right. But I managed to get inside. My mother was dying, and she needed a cure. I found out that the people of Welhair had the cure, but it was expensive for us to buy. I could pay for it if I had time to accumulate the fee, but my mother needed it immediately, so I broke into the fortress, found the vault, and took the cure for my mother. I would have got out too, but one guard walked into the vault and saw that the cures had been meddled with. He immediately raised the alarm. I managed to get out, though they chased me all the way to the borders. Luckily, they stopped at their borders, and I was able to travel more calmly. By the time I got home to my poor sick mother, she'd passed on. I was devastated, but there wasn't anything else I could do. I took the stolen cure to our doctor to give to the next person who needed it. Then I decided to get a job and earn the money for the cure. I would take the money back as a payment for what I had stolen."

"Strangely noble of you," Ethan pointed out.

John looked at him, surprised. "I didn't want to be a thief. I just didn't have any other option at the moment. Time was the trouble. I had asked the officials of Welhair to lend me the cure, but they refused. They didn't believe I would pay for it."

"You could have returned the cure to them."

"I know," John said with a short nod. "But they had a lot of it, and this one dose could be useful to someone else. Besides, it was better to wait a little while for them to cool down before I returned, and the cure wouldn't have lasted long enough. Money does last." They reached the forest near the castle and slowly continued up the hill. "I couldn't find any job in our village, so I continued up north," John continued. "Then I ran into this weird guy on the road. His coach had a smashed wheel. The horses were feeding on the grass, and the guy was sitting by the coach, reading a book. He looked so out of place in there. Somehow it felt as if he was waiting for me. He said that his coach had hit a bump, and the wheel had been damaged. He was alone and couldn't leave the coach and the horses, but he needed to take care of the wheel. So I offered to take the wheel to a nearby village and bring him a new one. But I needed money from him for the wheel. He gave me a huge amount of money. It would have been enough for the cure. It would have been enough for a new house too. He said he had no idea how much the wheel would cost, so I was to use as much money as I needed."

John continued, and a smile appeared on his face at this reminiscence. "I have to say it was tempting. I could have just gone to Welhair and paid for the cure. Or I could have kept the money and lived a nice life somewhere in the mountains. But I didn't want to leave the man stranded on the road, so I decided to figure out how to sort out the problem with the wheel first. I walked to the village and found the local blacksmith. He repaired the wheel and asked only for a small payment. When I came back with the wheel, I was, for a moment, tempted to say it had cost much more, but I returned the money and helped the guy to reinstall the wheel. Once we were finished, he asked me if I wanted a job. I said yes, and he took me to the headquarters of The League. That's the name we're using. I spent the next year in training. After the first year, I managed to save enough money, so I took a little trip to Welhair and paid for the cure. They were angry at first, but I explained my situation, and I think they understood why I had done what I did. They even looked sorry that my mum had died."

"What is this league?" Ethan asked, curious. He even slowed down to stay out of the castle bit longer. John was limping, and his left arm was hanging by his side. He didn't object to a slower pace.

"Our job is to keep magic at bay," John said after a short hesitation. "Some objects and beings are too powerful and can cause a lot of problems, as you probably know by now."

"So you were after Rex because he was that powerful?"

"Ehm … no," John said hesitantly. "I don't know the whole story there because it happened a few centuries ago. The League was already in place. There were two strong members—Fortis and Morgour. I don't know why he chose to use name Rex instead of Morgour here, but I suppose it was to hide his identity from us. They were getting on rather well, but they had some disagreements. One was on the purpose of The League. Fortis wanted to keep people of Lanland safe. Morgour thought that people were danger to themselves and The League should … do more than just keep them safe. He wanted to rule them. He believed that it was the only way to keep Lanland safe. Fortis disagreed with this.

"For a while it seemed that Morgour understood Fortis's point of view, and everything went smoothly. Then they had another disagreement over payment. Morgour believed that we should be getting some payment for our services. When someone needed our help, they should pay for it. Fortis was against this because a lot of people would have trouble paying. Most of the times we were not even called; instead, we simply reacted to strange situations. On top of that, we got a lot of weird objects out of our adventures, which was enough.

"Morgour pretended that he was okay with that—that he didn't mind that sort of payments as long as we were getting at least something. Then, at one point, he tried to gain control of Lanland using some of the objects we'd stored in our vault. He tried to kill Fortis but didn't succeed. He and Fortis were the strongest magical beings in The League, and so Morgour needed to get rid of the competition. Fortis was nearly defeated, but he managed to win. He trapped Morgour somewhere, but Morgour got out— or something. I'm not sure because Fortis doesn't talk about this, and Morgour tried to kill me right away, so I didn't have time to ask him about his history." John suddenly stopped and gasped, nearly falling down again. Ethan stopped too. "Ehm … could we sit down for a moment?" John asked.

Ethan looked around. Slowly and carefully he led John to the nearest tree and gently sat him down onto the ground. They were close to the castle, but there were still too many questions Ethan wanted to ask, so he decided to wait for John to rest a little. If necessary, he could run for help. John didn't object. He gratefully sat on the ground and leaned against the trunk of the tree, holding his ribs with his right hand. He closed his eyes and took a deep breath.

"Why did Rex come here?" Ethan asked as he sat on the ground.

John opened his eyes and looked at Ethan. "After their fight a few centuries ago, Morgour was no longer part of The League. I don't know how, but he escaped and went into hiding. Fortis looked for him, but Morgour was good at hiding. Fortis always said that Morgour wanted to dominate the world. Helping others was just a way for him to gain possession of various magical objects.

"Then about a hundred years ago, a strange earthquake happened in Wolfast. Fortis went to investigate. Normally, he would send someone—he rarely deals with things himself now—but this was no ordinary magic. He hired the man who owned the mines to find the stone. He tried to cover all the tracks to prevent Morgour from finding the stone. Once Fortis had possession of the stone, he knew that it was very powerful. It can guide or," John waved his hand in direction of Morgour's body, "control the minds of those around it. In the wrong hands, it could be dangerous."

"Why did Fortis leave the stone in Wolfast?" Ethan asked.

"It was his decision, and you'll have to ask him that question. I believe it was because he wanted to hide it. Morgour always thought that humans were the lowest creatures in the world—too weak even in comparison to animals and definitely too stupid. Fortis knew him. Morgour would look for the stone in many places, but not amongst humans. However, Morgour also knew Fortis, so it took him only a century to figure it all out.

"Fortis left the guardians of the stone with a communication device. After the device was activated, I came to check it out. And the stone was gone. I followed sources of information all the way to Royal City."

"Why didn't Fortis come himself?"

"He wasn't at headquarters when the call came. And at that time, we didn't know what was going on. They sent me because, as a human, I could blend in easily."

"How did you know so much about our knowledge of Rex? You knew that both Captain Stuart and Bess knew of Rex."

John smiled. "Captain Stuart was sending messages to you through Edmund when the werewolves were in the castle. He also gave some information to Edmund. And Edmund told me everything—about Bess being the only one who had actually met Rex and was still alive and about Rex's role in the whole war thing."

"But why did you stay in the city? Why didn't you—I don't know … look for Daniel?"

"I did! Right away," John said. He shrugged, and he winced at the pain and grabbed his ribs. He took a careful deep breath and then continued, "When I heard of a wolf that could change to a human after being bitten, I knew right away that we weren't dealing with a normal occurrence."

Ethan remembered the moment when he had talked to Daniel for the first time. Everyone thought that he was a werewolf, but he could hold a silver plate. And then they found out that Daniel was a wolf—a very articulate and smart wolf, even compared to most humans.

"That's why!" Ethan said, and he jumped to his feet, filled with excitement. "The necklace made Daniel smart! He was what he was because of it!" John nodded wearily, looking up at Ethan. Ethan looked at him and then frowned. "But why did I think it was a good idea to ask for his help?" he asked. Then the memory of the flash resurfaced. "The necklace made me?"

"It's very likely," John said calmly. "It also probably made those animals run from the forest and attack."

"No, they were replying to Bess's call."

"But the necklace made them want to reply. I mean, maybe. I don't … I don't know exactly. I didn't study the necklace, and I sure wouldn't be able to use it." He rubbed his eyes and looked around.

"Oh, we can probably continue," Ethan said, and he gently pulled John up. "You had a short rest here, so the rest of the path should be all right," he added. They walked in silence for a moment. Ethan was trying to work out all the information he had received. "So why didn't you follow Daniel?" he asked after a while.

"Because I saw him in the forest," John whispered. It seemed he was getting very tired. "I thought I would face a monster, but there was something very boyish about him. He seemed friendly and tame. And he didn't have the stone. I followed him for a mile to make absolutely sure. I wasn't sure if he had lost it during the fight, so I decided to return to the city. But it was difficult to get any information because, though I could move through the city and search for the stone, I had to lie low during the day, wasting my time.

"When I found out that Morgour's sidekick was in the city, I knew I had to get more information. She was looking for the stone. She even hired some local men. They had to be really scared, because they would rather fight me—or commit suicide by jumping off the roof in one case—than share any information with me. I knew I had to get into the city officially, so I manipulated Edmund to ask his friend's son to come to the city."

"How?" Ethan asked. He had an impression that John was human, so he had no special skills—save for the ability to climb houses and run across roofs.

"I had some special leaves. I could use them to plant ideas. They were just ideas, but if I chose a correct one, it would stick with a person. It was a small leaf. All I had to do was to come up with the idea and then make the leaf touch that person's skin. So I scared Edmund and then planted the idea that he could use an illustrator. I can draw and carve—my mother wanted me to become an artistic carver. So I knew I could do the job for The Royal Press and find out all I needed. I was a little nervous that it wouldn't work since The Royal Press didn't have an illustrator, but luckily

Edmund was ready for that change. I wasn't planning on staying longer than a few days. The Royal Press was kept informed on all official news, and my position gave me a potential opportunity to get to the lords.

"I found out about John Ericson, a friend of Edmunds, and his son, so I used him as a reference when I planted the idea in Edmund. Of course, I intercepted the letter and came in place of the boy. Will he be surprised if he receives requests for illustrations … But I had to come to the city! And being so close to an information source seemed like a good idea."

"Do you still have any of the leaves?"

"No." John shook his head. "I had only three. I used two leaves on Edmund—one for him to send for John Johnson and another to forgo the idea of illustrations. And I lost the last one in the city. When I was looking for it, Christine saw me. I thought of telling her the truth then and there, but a guard came, and I had to leave. I didn't want to hurt a member of the Royal Guards, and he surely would have fought me."

"You bumped into me in the Opera House on purpose?" Ethan asked.

John smiled wearily. "No, that was an accident. I'm sorry for that … and for not recognizing you," John added, looking at Ethan. "I wasn't expecting to meet you or see the necklace."

Ethan quickly reviewed the scenario in his head. "That's why you were so surprised when you saw the necklace," he said. "I thought that it was a standard reaction. People were always in awe when they saw the necklace, but to you, it had to be a real surprise."

"I was startled for a moment," John admitted. "I didn't expect to encounter the stone so quickly. And then Christine came, and I found out that you were the king."

"Why didn't you visit me at home that night? Why wait?"

"There was one thing I didn't anticipate when I came here officially: that other people would know of me too and would count on me. I shook off Christine quickly. First, I went after the attacker. I knew he had some information, and I knew where to start looking for him. I caught up with your attacker, but he chose to jump off the roof. He landed right in front of Christine. She sprinted in the opposite direction from her home. I realized she wanted to hide at my place, so I rushed back there. I needed to protect my identity until I could get the necklace. I had to hide my clothes, and I was in such a hurry, I couldn't find my nightgown. When she arrived, I had to pretend I had been asleep to cover up why it had taken me so long to answer her knock. It was too late to come to see you afterwards."

"Wait a minute," Ethan said with a frown. He looked down at John's coat, which looked waterproof and heavy. He remembered the hat, which had been strong and big. "When I saw you in the opera house, you were wearing normal clothes. The attacker chose to impersonate you, so he was wearing the same clothes you are wearing now—even the hat. Yet when he died, he wasn't dressed like that, and you were dressed like this."

"He had similar clothes," John corrected Ethan. "These were a gift from my boss. They are normal clothes, but they can shrink to the size of a small handkerchief. I was carrying them all the time, and if I needed to check something incognito, I would just take them out and put them on. As for your attacker, he threw off the cloak and hat as soon as he left the opera house."

Ethan thought about that for a moment and then nodded. "Okay," he said, "that was the first night, but you came much later."

"Suddenly, there was someone more important to me than you or the necklace," John said, his speech slowing down. "I realized this in a few days when I was waiting for Christine at The Royal Press. I had taken some precautions, but I was already too late."

They continued in silence. Ethan was trying to process all the information and put together the big picture. They reached the drawbridge and entered the castle grounds. A few doctors were running among the injured guards and citizens. Lord Thomas was helping one of the doctors, still wearing his bear costume, but without the nose and the hat. Ethan was glad that he had spent the evening in the castle. That had kept him out of harm's way.

Ethan looked around, searching for others. Captain Stuart was limping on top of the castle walls, giving out orders. He was barking at the guards much more than was necessary. His limping seemed to have got much worse. Lord Adrian wasn't far away, but he was busy with some guards by the gate. Ethan assumed that Lord Charles was still outside the castle grounds.

"We're nearly there," Ethan said. He looked at John, who was very pale. "You can tell me why you came to my chambers with a knife," he said, trying to keep John awake. He needed him to walk to the hospital ward. He hoped that, if he could keep him distracted, John could hold on. And, as a bonus, Ethan could find out more information in case John didn't make it. "I know that you didn't want to harm me, but that visit was very suspicious. Or was it you?"

"It was," John whispered. His voice was getting weaker with every step. Ethan continued with John towards the castle, walking around guards lying on the ground, awaiting doctors. Ethan was sure that Captain Stuart or Lord Adrian had set up a hospital ward inside the castle.

"I knew by then that you had the … the necklace," John continued. He was moving more and more sluggishly. Ethan wasn't sure how long John could hold up. "I wanted … " John coughed and winced at the pain. "I wanted to get it. I had a knife because … because Rex's henchmen also … also … " John's breath caught in his throat. Lord Adrian noticed Ethan and waved at him. Ethan nodded to Lord Adrian, half leading, half dragging John towards the castle. "They realized that you had it and came to the castle … " John continued. "I had to kill them … I had to. Otherwise … they would have killed you."

"But they attacked me in the opera house. They had to know that I had it by then. Why did they wait? For you?"

John shook his head. More of his weight fell on Ethan, and for a moment Ethan thought that John had fainted. "No," John whispered. "I have only a theory … about what happened since Robert … didn't want to talk about it, and he … jumped … off the roof. I believe he saw you getting out of the coach at the opera house and saw the necklace … That's why he went after … you." John stopped and coughed vigorously. Ethan saw that Lord Adrian was walking towards them.

"Keep your strength," Ethan said. "You will tell me this later."

John shook his head and took a deep breath. "I might not get the chance," he said weakly, and he stepped forward. They finally reached the gate of the castle and entered. Lord Adrian started to run. "Robert didn't have time … " John gasped but quickly continued, "to inform any of his colleagues … and soon afterwards I found him and he … killed himself, so not even … Rex's sidekick knew what—" John stopped abruptly. "I don't feel good," he said wearily, and Ethan nearly fell beneath his weight. Frantically, Ethan looked around. He needed help. All of John's weight was leaning against him. He had to stop John from falling to the ground. Lord Adrian appeared by his side.

"Your Majesty," Lord Adrian breathed out. "Thank the gods you are all right."

"I'm fine," Ethan said. "Please, help me with John," he added, feeling that John was slipping from his grasp. He hoped that John had only fainted. Lord Adrian immediately took John's other arm and put it around his shoulders. Ethan expected John to scream with pain, but nothing happened. "I think he fainted," Ethan said, trying to see John's face. "Hurry!"

With this, he half walked, half ran through the castle. Lord Adrian was moving fast, taking most of John's weight upon himself. Lord Adrian didn't talk as they carried John inside, and Ethan was too busy looking around him. There were only a few guards inside the castle, mostly carrying patients to the hospital ward. Lord Adrian led the way to the second floor ballroom where temporary beds had been set up.

As soon as they entered the hall, two doctors jumped to their feet and hurried towards them. They led them to a bed in the corner, and Ethan and Lord Adrian carefully put John down. Ethan leaned against the wall, partially to catch his breath, but mainly to wait for the doctors' verdict.

"What was that blow?" Lord Adrian asked, as he stood next to Ethan. The doctors took off John's shirt and checked his ribs.

"I don't know," Ethan said. "We'll hopefully find that out once John wakes up. I'm sure glad that it's all over. How's Bess doing?"

"He died soon after that blow shook the castle. I didn't let them bury him. I'm not an expert on werewolves, so when everything calmed down, I asked Joan to hurry into the library and find any available information—mainly, how long it takes for a werewolf to wake up. I wouldn't like to bury him too soon. Though the arrow missed his heart, and it wasn't silver, so technically, he should wake up. She's now checking the books."

Ethan was tempted to ask how Joan was doing, but when he opened his mouth, no sound came. Lord Adrian looked at him sideways and then lowered his voice.

"She's a little mess," he said as if reading Ethan's mind. Ethan didn't say anything. He was mad at her for lying to him, but a little part of him felt bad. Lord Adrian's words stung at his heart.

"We have a lot to do," Ethan said. He spun around and marched out of the ward, completely forgetting about John.

CHAPTER 13

Christine collapsed onto the ground, sobbing. She had run out of the castle an hour ago, searching for John. No one knew where John was, and she couldn't find him anywhere. She was exhausted and out of breath. Tears were running down her cheeks as fear overtook her.

"Are you all right, miss?" a familiar voice asked her.

She looked up. Leaning above her, stood the guard she had already met twice—once when he went to the inn to stop the fight, and again when he had escorted her home. She was glad to see him. She wiped the tear off her cheek and opened her mouth. Her throat felt tight; it wouldn't let any sound out. She wasn't even sure what she wanted to say. On the one hand, she wanted to know if John was all right; on the other, she was scared that he wasn't.

The guard knelt down to bring his face to level with Christine's. "Are you hurt?" he asked her. Christine shook her head. She gulped, her eyes filling with tears once again. "What's wrong?" the guard asked her patiently.

"I'm looking for someone," she said in a muffled voice. "He was holding a glass shield and fighting here."

"I know! I saw him," the guard said with a short nod. "He should now be in the temporary hospital in the castle." Christine staggered to her feet, her heart racing. The guard stood up. "The king himself took him there. They were walking slowly, but they should be there already."

Christine hadn't dared to hope. She watched the guard for a while, lost for words. Then she spun around and sprinted towards the castle.

"Check the ballroom!" the guard shouted after her. She didn't slow down. She continued running uphill towards the silhouette of the castle. She didn't stop even when she ran out of breath. She had a painful stabbing pain in her side when she finally reached the drawbridge, and she had to stop for a moment to let the pain pass. Then she continued on to the yard, still fighting for her breath. She ran into the castle and sprinted up the stairs, taking two at a time. She continued all the way to the second floor. Four stairs from the top, she fell down on all fours and crawled to the top. There she sat down because black spots appeared in her vision. She sat on the cold stone, panting, until her vision returned. She staggered to her feet and half walked, half dragged her feet to the ballroom. Finally, she reached the big hall and stopped at the threshold. She leaned against the doorframe and looked around.

There were made up beds all around the hall filled with guards. She wasn't sure where to start. She looked around, searching for John. After what seemed like forever, she spotted him in the corner to her left. She walked between the beds, avoiding the doctors. No one paid her any attention. She reached John's bed and froze. He was lying on his back, covered with blanket. His hands were lying by his side. He had bandages on his chest and left shoulder. He also had many scratches on his face and hands. His eyes were closed, and his mouth slightly open. He would have looked peaceful if it hadn't been for his erratic breathing and the sweat on his forehead.

She thought she would scream at him, even slap him for lying to her, but seeing him there so helpless, she couldn't stay mad at him. She sat down on the edge of the bed, hoping that the movement would wake him up.

"Do you know him, ma'am?" a female's voice said above Christine. She looked up into a doctor's face. The doctor stood there with a bowl in her hands.

"He's a—a friend," Christine said. "Will he be all right?"

"It's too soon to tell," the doctor said, and she placed the bowl next to Christine. "He has a fever. His shoulder was dislocated. We managed to put it back, but it will take a while for the shoulder to heal. He has also four broken ribs. There is some tissue damage in his chest as well as in his back, not to mention his shoulder. And he's exhausted."

"Can I do something?" Christine asked, watching John's restless face.

"You can cool down his face," the doctor said. She handed Christine a cloth. "If the water gets too warm, find me, and I'll give you more cold water."

152

Christine nodded and took the cloth. She put it into the ice-cold water and wrung it into the bowl. The doctor left her, walking to the other side of the room. Christine placed the cloth on John's forehead. John jerked and opened his eyes. He looked at Christine, who smiled. "Hi," she whispered, keeping the cloth on John's forehead. "How are you feeling?"

"Hi," John whispered back with a weak smile. "I feel like I've fallen off a four-storey building or have been fighting all night with broken ribs. Were you waiting for me to wake up?"

"Sort of," Christine admitted. She took the cloth off John's forehead and put it into the bowl. "I just wonder why you didn't tell me the truth," she said to the bowl as she wrung out the cloth again.

"I didn't want to put you in danger," John said.

"That's why you pretended to leave the city?" she asked as she looked at him. She felt like crying but fought back the tears.

"Yes. And also because I realized that I cared more for you than anything else," John whispered as she placed the cloth on his forehead. She looked him in the eye. "I had to leave," John continued, "before our relationship became too painful. I was sent here, and there's no knowing where they'll send me next. I didn't want to confuse you. And I definitely didn't want to cause you any pain."

"You saved us, so I suppose it would be stupid of me to be completely mad with you," Christine said with a smile. John chuckled and winced at the pain. "Yet, I wish you had told me," she added. "I could have been of help to you."

"You were," John said.

Christine pressed her lips together. "Yes, I know," she said coldly. "You used my information without telling me. You used me."

"No," John whispered and shook his head.

Christine lifted the cloth off his forehead. "You used my informers, too," she said. "That's why you stayed longer, isn't it? When I told you I had an informer, you wanted to meet him. And you threw Tim out of that window so that he would answer your questions."

"No!" John said louder, and he closed his eyes. A painful grimace crossed his face. Christine narrowed her eyes but stayed quiet. "I didn't throw Tim out of the window," John whispered. "He fell. I swear. I just took a little bit of time to pull him inside. I wouldn't have hurt him. He wasn't trying to kill anyone, and he wasn't dangerous. I just used the situation."

"Yes, as you used me to get information."

"No," John once again shook his head. There was urgency in his voice. "No information from you ... well, except that Rex was already in the city ... " John hesitated and then shook his head. "I could have done without information from you. But the only thing that made me keep going during that fight was the thought of you. There were many moments when I wanted to give up. I felt like fainting from pain on multiple occasions, but I knew that, if I did, you would be in danger. And I wanted to tell you I was sorry. Thinking of you gave me strength."

Any remnant of anger that may have been inside Christine vanished. She could feel warmth on her face. A smile spread on her face. She put the cloth back onto his forehead and looked him in the eye. "You were really getting on my nerves in the beginning," she said reproachfully.

"I wanted to keep my distance, so I tried to do things I had noticed were annoying to you. But then ... " John stopped and smiled. "After a little while I wanted to make a good impression on you."

"By that giggling?" Christine asked as she lifted the cloth from his forehead and put it into the bowl. She was surprised at how warm the cloth was.

John laughed and winced. "I really giggle like an idiot sometimes," he admitted. "You're not the only one who has told me that. Though I admit I used that giggle much more than I usually do. I hoped that it would drive you mad."

"It didn't go according to the plan, did it?"

"No," John admitted. "I needed to check where the necklace was. Using The Royal Printer seemed like a good idea at the time." Christine looked at him while she wrung the cloth into the bowl. "I thought that I would just go to the ball and then vanish afterwards, especially when I found the necklace. But you were worried, and I didn't want to blow my cover. I tried to convince myself that I was staying near you because you had connections, but the truth was that I didn't need your connections. I already knew where the necklace was. I just wanted to be close to you. I realized this when I nearly kissed you at my place. I realized that your safety had become more important to me than the safety of the world. I hadn't wanted to make any friends here, and I sure hadn't expected to fall in love."

Christine blushed. She looked him in the eye. John didn't say anything; he just met her stare. They stayed still for a moment, looking at each other, and then Christine leaned in and gently kissed John on lips. John kissed her back. He took a deep breath as their lips touched and winced at the pain. Christine quickly straightened up. John had his eyes closed. There was a painful grimace on his face. Slowly, he opened his eyes again and looked at Christine. He smiled at her through the pain.

"Just get better," Christine said as she put the cloth on his forehead. "That's all I want right now."

John smiled and closed his eyes. Christine kept on cooling down the cloth, until John fell asleep again. His breathing became calmer and more regular. She didn't want to leave his side, so the doctors brought her a blanket. She fell asleep on the floor by John's bed but wouldn't have changed that for the softest bed in the world.

Lord Adrian entered the library. Joan was sitting by a table that was covered with books. She was asleep, using one book as a pillow. Lord Adrian closed the door of the library. Though he tried to be as quiet as possible, the door closed with a click. Joan jumped with start and looked around surprised. "Lord Adrian!" she said when she spotted him. "What time is it?"

"It's after midnight," Lord Adrian said quietly, stepping closer. "Maybe you should go to bed. I have prepared another room for you next to your old quarters. It's much smaller, but that's the best I can do right now. I will let you know once we clean up your former quarters."

Joan shook her head and closed the book in front of her. "Thank you for the room. I will use it tonight, but I will leave tomorrow morning."

"Please, stay one more night," Lord Adrian said. Joan looked up at him and shook her head. Her eyes were red and swollen. "Please," he said. "If nothing changes, I will arrange a coach for you."

Tears filled Joan's eyes. She smiled feebly and turned to the books on the table. "I've checked the information," she said, her voice trembling. Lord Adrian felt that she was trying to change the subject. "Werewolves do wake up after several hours, depending on the injury. The werewo—the leader of Wolfast should be up before dawn if I understood this correctly." She pointed at the book she had used as a pillow.

"That's wonderful news," Lord Adrian said, picking up another book. It was called *History of Wolfast*. "Thank you so much for your help." Joan nodded and stood up. "Please, promise me you will stay at least one day."

"The king wouldn't want me to stay," Joan pointed out. Lord Adrian pressed his lips together. He couldn't argue with that. "I should leave as soon as possible," Joan added.

"I understand how you feel," Lord Adrian said. Joan looked at him. "I'm asking you to stay just one more day." Joan shook her head. "Then stay till lunch. Either the king will ask you to stay, or I will provide you with a comfortable coach for your journey back home."

Joan smiled feebly. "The king won't lend me any of his coaches," she whispered.

"I already told you that I have a lot of privileges," Lord Adrian said with a smile. "This is one of them."

Joan sighed, and after a short hesitation, she nodded. She started to place the books in a pile, avoiding Lord Adrian's stare. "Please, take some rest. It was a difficult night for all of us," Lord Adrian said, taking the books out of Joan's hands.

"Thank you," she whispered, and she quickly left the library, avoiding Lord Adrian's stare. Lord Adrian watched after her, deep in thought. Then he looked at all the books in his hands. On the table was a piece of paper filled with notes Joan had recorded from the books. It was a long list. Joan had put a lot of work into this.

CHAPTER 14

E than returned to his quarters five hours later, after he had checked everything that needed his attention, including some things that could have waited. He'd had to change his clothes during the night because, when a doctor was treating the wound on his forehead, another doctor had slipped and sent a whole bowl of cold water all over Ethan. Ethan wasn't mad and had a hard time explaining to the second doctor that he needn't apologize anymore.

Now he was glad because at least he was now wearing clean clothes, and when he reached his bed, he fell down onto soft pillows with a clear conscience. An idea that he should clean up, change, or at least take off his shoes crossed his mind, but he was out cold before he could even think, *Oh, what the heck.*

He woke up in a few hours feeling completely beaten up. It was already after dawn, and the sun was shining into the room. At first he wondered what had happened. Then the memories flooded in with every painful moment of the previous night. First he remembered death of Lord James. He moaned and rubbed his forehead, wincing at the pain from his wound. He pushed back the thought that another family line had died now, and he was once again one lord short.

Lord James's face flashed in front of his eyes with that grin of his. Ethan remembered that day when they had fought for the castle, and Lord James had caused panic in the yard. He remembered how Lord James had sneaked out of the camp and singlehandedly taken the cart full of food and weapons from Blake's men, killing most of them. He remembered the story of Lord James's life. Norenians didn't believe in an afterlife, but it used to be part of their culture in the past. He liked to imagine Lord

James meeting with the love of his life in heaven. They both would deserve that for sure.

Memories, one after another, flashed into his mind—the day when Ethan was five, and they met for the first time. Ethan could still remember how Lord James patted his head. Lord James was never much for traditions, and he sure didn't care about etiquette. Funny how things change. Lord James had gone from a gentleman to a pirate and then to a lord who won respect of the people of Norene and the soldiers of Wolfast.

Then Daniel's face resurfaced. Ethan groaned and stood up. It was tougher to not think about Daniel. He paced the room for a moment, trying to suppress the memories, but it was useless. He spun around and barged outside. He marched through the anteroom and opened the door swiftly. He nearly crashed into Lord Adrian, who was about to knock on his door.

"Good morning," Lord Adrian said in surprise. "There is a strange … phenomenon on the horizon, Your Majesty. I thought you might want to see it."

Ethan looked at Lord Adrian, and his imagination immediately supplied him with an image of a huge storm with strange foggy aura rushing towards the castle with puppet-like people behind it. He hurried around Lord Adrian without a single word. Lord Adrian followed him immediately. Ethan ran through the castle, imagining every possible scenario.

"I also have the report on last night if you wish to hear it," Lord Adrian said behind him, having a hard time keeping up.

Ethan sighed. He wasn't sure how much bad news he could handle. Then again, not knowing was probably worse. "Tell me," he said wearily, and he slowed down so Lord Adrian could catch up with him.

Lord Adrian looked at the papers in his hand. "The aftermath isn't actually that bad, considering the situation," he said. "We have a hundred and seventeen dead guards and over a hundred injured. A hundred and two guards fell on Rex's side. They weren't protecting themselves, and Rex didn't care. I'm not counting Lord James and Daniel. Their bodies were both taken to the crypt beneath the castle." They reached the stairs and started to descend. "The official funeral of Lord James is planned for tomorrow. It will be held in the fields between the castle and the city at sunset. I think Daniel should be there too. As for the civilians, we have only twenty-two dead and five wounded. They either got to the safety of the castle or stayed in their homes. The guards managed to control the situation in the city before we lost it."

Ethan felt pride rise inside him. Norene had the best soldiers in whole of Lanland as far as he was concerned. "What about the property?" he asked.

"There is no significant damage of property," Lord Adrian said calmly as they entered the ballroom. Ethan hurried through the hall, avoiding the beds and the doctors. "There is some damage to Lord Thomas's palace, mainly plaster on the facade. Luckily the whole battle took place in the fields. Unfortunately, our wildlife is damaged. Many animals were killed. I don't know the impact on the surrounding nature yet."

Ethan stepped onto the balcony and stopped. Lord Adrian stopped behind him, consulting the papers in his hands again. The last time Ethan was on this balcony, Joan had refused his proposal. Even after all that had happened, that memory stung him a little.

Bess stood by the rails, watching the horizon. He was wearing the same suit of clothes he'd worn the previous night. It was stained with dirt, grass, and blood. He looked from the horizon to Ethan and bowed his head slightly. Ethan bowed his head back, and Bess turned back to the horizon. Ethan also turned his focus on the horizon. He walked to the rails, looking at the white line moving towards the castle. At first he was at loss, but then he realized that he was looking at people in white uniforms. They were walking in the direction of the castle. Their shields were so polished that they shone. Three men on white horses were in the lead.

Bess looked at Ethan and then back at the white line in front of him. "Do you have any idea what that is?" he asked. Lord Adrian stopped next to Ethan and shrugged.

Ethan squinted at the white line. "I think that is the army John mentioned," he said. "They came at last."

"After the fight," Lord Adrian pointed out.

"It's good to know that we would have had backup if Rex managed to push us into the castle," Ethan said. "We could have held him off for a few days in here."

"Good thing it didn't come to that," Bess said quietly. Ethan nodded absentmindedly.

"The weirdest part is that the army just appeared there," Lord Adrian said, watching the horizon. "We weren't informed of its approach."

Ethan looked at Lord Adrian and then back at the army. Seeing the army there reminded him of John. "How's John doing?" Ethan asked Lord Adrian.

Lord Adrian looked at him and shook his head. "I don't know," he said. "He was sleeping after midnight when I came to check up on him. I haven't checked this morning. With Lord James gone, there's a huge part of the castle's security that needs covering. Captain Stuart is doing a great job at the moment, but we're just finding out how much James actually did around here."

Ethan nodded slowly. He had wanted to leave his bedroom to stop thinking about death of his friends, but it was coming back when he least expected it to. Ethan turned around and walked towards the ballroom. "There are still some things that need to get solved," he said to Lord Adrian, who immediately stepped after him. "I would like to use Bess's visit to negotiate peace. And I've been thinking a lot about our army. Part of the army consists of the Royal Guards, and that segment is stronger than ever, but there are still soldiers from Blake who haven't joined the Royal Guards, and now with Lord James and Lord Eric gone, there is a whole fleet of ships."

"We're running out of lords," Lord Adrian said. Ethan stopped by the stairs and turned to face him.

"No we're not," he said. "There are still families who have remained. Lord Eric did have two daughters ... three daughters," he added. He could feel the blood rushing to his face.

"I know this isn't my place," Lord Adrian said timidly, "but I think you should discuss this with Joan. She's a remarkable woman, and she never lied about herself. She just didn't tell the whole truth."

"You're right," Ethan snapped. "It isn't your place."

"My apologies," Lord Adrian said with a small bow. "You were saying that Lord Eric had only daughters and no sons."

"Yes," Ethan said slowly and shook his head. Joan was strangely still occupying his thoughts. "Yes, he had daughters. And also Lord Jonathan had a sister. She's very smart. I've been thinking about this for some time now," he said. Suddenly, he realized that Joan had made him re-evaluate their laws. She was smart and well educated. There was no reason why a woman couldn't inherit the duties. He shook his head and pushed Joan to the back of his mind once again. "I've been thinking about changing the law that dictates that only a male heir can inherit the lordship. I would change it to 'the heir'—not male or female."

"Women are part of our culture," Lord Adrian said. "They are proving to be excellent in dealing with just about anything, and in some cases they are better at solving problems than men are. But are you sure they could take on lordly responsibilities?"

"We educate women the same way we educate man," Ethan said. "There are some men who don't really progress. This doesn't mean that men are stupid. We should treat women the same way. We should judge people based on their actions, not their gender. If we were dealing with the loss of one lord, I wouldn't think about this so much, but this way, we can still have four more families in the council. Without the change, I would have three lords only—one of whom is completely new to the roll. Seven is a better number. Besides, women can bring some interesting ideas we wouldn't think of."

"I think that your decision will cause a lot of fuss, but in the circumstances, it's the best one even I can think of."

Ethan looked at Lord Adrian, nodding slowly. He knew that his decision wouldn't go without comments. However, Ethan had high hopes for Norene, especially after he had learned about Lord James's story. "I'm sure this is the right choice," he said resolutely.

Ethan looked over Lord Adrian's shoulder and spotted John and Christine. They were slowly walking towards them. Lord Adrian turned around and looked at them too. John looked terrible. In addition to the healing cuts, there were multiple bruises on his hands and his neck. He looked in pain as he gingerly walked towards them. He was limping, using Christine's arm for support. Ethan realized that, when Rex attacked the dome, it held up only thanks to John's willpower and strength.

"Good morning," Ethan said. John looked up and smiled through his pain. The result was a grimace. "I assume you saw the approaching army," Ethan added. John nodded shortly, twitching as he did so. "Do you need any help?" Ethan asked, watching John walk gingerly forward.

"No," John whispered, shaking his head as he and Christine walked by Ethan. "The broken ribs are causing me a lot of trouble right now, but luckily I don't need to fight anymore."

Ethan smiled and slowly followed John and Christine down the stairs and out of the castle. Lord Adrian walked next to Ethan, deep in thought. When they stepped into the yard, the murmuring stopped, and complete silence fell. The guards stepped aside to let them walk through, saluting John. John blushed as he slowly moved down towards the castle wall. He looked a little embarrassed as he nodded his thanks to the guards.

They stopped near the gate, John leaning against Christine's shoulder. Ethan walked around them and looked up at the walls. Captain Stuart watched them. As soon as Ethan looked up, Captain Stuart called from the walls: "Only one man on a horse approached the gate, Your Majesty!"

"Let him in!" Ethan shouted back.

The drawbridge was lowered, and the gate was lifted. Ethan saw a young man sitting on a white horse. His white tunic over his silver armour shone in comparison with the dark stone and green grass. It looked like he was bringing light with him. The stranger entered the castle and jumped down from his horse in the yard. He looked around, his gaze momentarily stopping on John. He had brown eyes, but the moment he laid his eyes on John, the colour changed to bright blue. Ethan looked at John, who stood with his eyes closed, his jaw tight, leaning against Christine. Ethan looked at the stranger whose eyes were once again brown. Ethan wasn't sure if he had imagined the colour change or not. The stranger approached Ethan and bowed his head.

"Thank you for coming here," Ethan said. "I believe that you're responding to John's call."

The man looked at John and then back at Ethan. "I believe so," he said. "My name is Fortis and ... John ... called us to help with Rex. However, I can see that our help would have been too late if it was needed at all. For this I would like to apologize."

"Well ... " Ethan started, tempted to flood Fortis with all the questions he had. "Thank you," he said uncertainly instead.

"We would like to ask you for a favour," Fortis said, and his polite voice changed to more matter-of-fact tone. "We want to take Rex's body with us. It contains the gem which might cause you more trouble if it remained in Norene."

"How would you get it out of … No, don't tell me," Ethan said as he rubbed the bridge of his nose. Weird images flashed in front of his eyes. He pushed them aside. The images were immediately replaced by a flood of questions. Who was this man? Where had he come from? Why hadn't there been any forewarning that an army like that was approaching? What was the stone? What would Fortis do with it? Why had Daniel died? Why had Rex controlled the stone? Why and what and how … so many questions.

"I believe that you have some questions about the events of the last few months," Fortis said. Ethan looked up at him. There was an understanding smile on Fortis's face as he watched Ethan's internal struggle. "I'm sorry for all the trouble Rex caused," Fortis continued, "though I'm impressed at how you managed to deal with it. I wish I could have had a go at him. We were old acquaintances. The most important thing is that it's over now, and he won't cause any more trouble."

"What are you?" Ethan blurted out. He hadn't meant to ask the question; it had just slipped out.

Fortis smiled and looked at John, who watched the scene with a tired look on his face. "I'm a member of—"

"The League, I know," Ethan said with a wave of his hand. "I meant *what* are you?" He could see that Lord Adrian, Christine, and most of the guards around them were surprised, as if he had asked a very strange question. However, some nodded slowly in agreement, and John shifted uneasily. "I might be wrong," Ethan admitted, "but you are no human being. Neither was Rex. And you are not a werewolf."

"And neither was Rex," Fortis finished. He smiled and tilted his head a little. A strange feeling ran through Ethan's body. It wasn't fear; it was a realization that Rex might not have been too different from this being. How dangerous was the man in front of him?

"There are many creatures in Lanland," Fortis said. "In the past, you have met only werewolves, but there are many different magical and non-magical beings around you. I'm from far, far south—the other end of the world, as some say. My island and all of my kin are no longer part of this world, and now that Rex is dead, I'm the last one."

"How old are you?" Ethan asked.

Fortis smiled wearily. "Very old indeed," he said.

"Are you immortal?" Lord Adrian asked, folding his arms.

"In a way," Fortis said, slightly turning to Lord Adrian. "In some ways, I am like the werewolves. You can kill me, but I won't die of old age. That wasn't normal for my kin. There was a dead volcano on our island that contained nearly all the magical stones in Lanland. We dug them out throughout the centuries, looking for the powerful ones. But somehow we forgot about the volcano. There were small earthquakes on the island. They happened so often and they were so small that we no longer noticed them. We had no idea that they were caused by the volcano. And one day, the volcano blew up.

"The stones had been stored in a cave inside the volcano, and when the lava hit, they exploded. Morgour and I wanted to get them out, but we were too late. We rushed into the caves, and the eruption knocked me unconscious. I woke up on a beach on the mainland a day later. At first, I tried to find anyone from the island, but the island had vanished and so had the people. After a while, I realized I wasn't getting any older. A combination of the stones probably changed me; the same way the necklace changed Daniel. Well … not the same way. For me it was a blast."

"So you could control the gems if you wanted to," Ethan said.

"Not really," Fortis said. "There's still too much we don't know about the gems. But we found out that magma is hot enough to destroy them. My kin believed that there were no more magical gems outside the island, but I felt that this was not the case. I think there are stones throughout the whole of Lanland. I wanted to find them, but so did Morgour."

"John said that he used to work for The League," Ethan pointed out.

"Yes." Fortis nodded. His jaw tightened, and his features hardened. Ethan had an urge to step back. "When we found each other, about twenty years after the volcano woke up, we were both happy. I wanted to use our knowledge and abilities for good, but Morgour wanted to find other gems. We had—we still have—no idea how many are there. Maybe this was the only one; maybe there are hundreds. I genuinely thought that he wanted to help, but he was only using us. We got some additional information about a possible gem, and that's when Morgour chose to show his true face. I wasn't ready for that, but I survived the attack. Morgour managed to escape in the end, and he hid for centuries. I looked for him, but he was careful. I'm glad it's all over, but I would really have liked to have faced him. It doesn't matter now, though."

Fortis turned to John and beckoned for him to come closer. John stepped forward, but Christine grabbed his arm. He turned around and smiled at her reassuringly. Christine let him go, looking tormented. John limped to Fortis and hung his head. His hands were shaking. Ethan had no idea why John was so nervous when he had done such a great job of protecting them all.

"I've been thinking about your next appointment," Fortis said. John nodded, and Christine covered her face. Ethan understood their nervousness. This was the moment when they would have to say goodbye. "Since there's been so much trouble here, it's our duty to make sure that everything gets back to normal." John lifted his head, watching Fortis unbelievingly. "And by the look of it, you could do with extended recovery. For a long time, I have wanted to expand our informer network to the North Sea." A smile appeared on John's face. Christine looked at them through her fingers. "Therefore, I would like you to remain in Norene indefinitely."

"Thank you, sir." John breathed out his words and stepped back. Christine clapped her hands over her mouth, her eyes shining with happiness. John turned to her, beaming, and she jumped towards him. She threw herself into John's arms, and John staggered under her weight. He nearly fell to the ground as Christine jumped back, startled. John looked pale, and a hesitant smile appeared on his face. Fortis turned away from them with a satisfied smile on his face.

Ethan watched them with a frown. He knew that John had lied to Christine about what and who he was, yet she didn't look as if she minded now. Then again, John had probably done so to protect her; he hadn't wanted to pull her into the fight, even though she had already been involved.

"You seem lost in your thoughts," Fortis said to Ethan. Ethan turned his focus on this strange visitor. Fortis was watching Ethan with an amused expression on his face. Ethan shrugged and turned his back to John and Christine. Fortis stepped towards the castle walls, and Ethan followed him, not really paying attention to their surroundings.

"There are just some things I don't understand," Ethan said. "No one knew what John was. Christine had no idea and yet …"

"Are you wondering why she would forgive his lie?" Fortis asked. Ethan looked at him and shrugged. "It's really difficult to answer," Fortis said with a sigh. "I think your first question should be: why did John lie in the first place? That is, if he really lied."

"What do you mean?"

"Sometimes we don't say the whole truth; sometimes intentionally, sometimes unintentionally. Though it's not really a lie, it can hurt just the same. So what was the motive?"

"He wanted to protect her?" Ethan offered.

"Do you believe that?"

"Ehm … no, not really," Ethan admitted. "I think he was trying to protect himself, at least at the beginning."

"Maybe," Fortis said thoughtfully, and he put his hands behind his back. Ethan realized they were all alone. Fortis had that rare ability to empty out a place without saying a single word. People just felt when they should leave him alone. "Do you think she is wrong in forgiving him?"

"Yes," Ethan said without thinking. "He lied. He might have avoided direct question, or maybe there was no direct question, but he should have told her, 'Look, I'm the Masked Man'."

"Why?"

"So she would know not to fall for him."

"We can't plan falling in love," Fortis pointed out. Ethan grunted. "We're not really talking about John and Christine, are we?" Fortis asked calmly and stopped.

Ethan stopped and turned towards him. He was in no mood to tell him about Joan. It was no one else's business.

"I don't know whom we're talking about," Fortis said calmly when Ethan hadn't said anything, "but you should ask yourself whether it's a true betrayal. Sometimes we do stupid things when we're in love. Trust me, I know."

Ethan looked into Fortis's eyes, thinking hard. Maybe it would be worthwhile to discuss this with Joan without any emotions or accusations. She had told him not to call her lady. She just hadn't clarified why, and Ethan assumed that, like him, she didn't like ceremony.

"Look at it from this point of view," Fortis continued. "You can ask me any question you want, yet we're talking about this person. Obviously she's important to you. That has to mean something."

Ethan froze. Once again at the mention of Joan, he completely forgot everything else. He cleared his throat and looked at Fortis. "May I still ask you other questions?" he asked.

"Fire away," Fortis said with a smile.

"Rex was using a fog, and he was able to control anyone who entered it," Ethan said. Fortis nodded. "Yet when Daniel fell into the fog … Daniel is—"

"I know," Fortis said calmly. "Norene and Wolfast were discussing Daniel's existence in detail. I knew right away that this had something to do with the necklace."

"Okay … so, Daniel fell into the fog, but he wasn't affected by it. He walked all the way to Rex and then attacked him. There was a blow. Daniel didn't survive it. I don't understand why. He was a werewolf—sort of. He should have survived that."

"Even if Daniel were a real werewolf, he wouldn't have survived it," Fortis said grimly. "I did some study regarding the necklace. It lives its own life. It can manipulate those around it—even the reality around it. It usually uses that power to keep itself safe. However, Rex was strong enough to control it. That manipulation is actually rather difficult, so not anyone could have done it. I assume that Rex quickly managed to get lightning under control—maybe not from the very first moment, but after a bit of practice." Ethan nodded. "With his death," Fortis continued, "all that power he was building inside him was released. Those who were closest to him didn't stand a chance."

"I still don't understand why Daniel died. He survived many things. He should have survived that experience."

"It's not something that happens a lot," Fortis said slowly, "but electricity can kill a werewolf. The probability of a lightning hitting a werewolf is small; especially because they hate being out in the rain. You could say that the lightning has the same effect as fire. No werewolf stands a chance against that."

"And why didn't the fog control Daniel?"

"Rex thought that he knew everything there was to know about the stone. He was obsessed with it, true, but that's not enough to know everything. He either underestimated the stone or overestimated his own powers. He thought that he could control it completely by making it part of him. Once the stone was inside him, he had better control of its powers, but he still couldn't control it completely."

"What would happen if he … you know … " Ethan waved his hand, trying to find correct words.

"If he had defecated it?" Fortis asked with a smile. Ethan nodded. Fortis's eyes momentarily turned blue. It was only for a fraction of a second, but Ethan knew that he hadn't imagined it this time. "I guess we'll never find out," Fortis said. "I can imagine one scenario, but I don't want to go into too much detail. Of course, there's also the possibility that he would have … digested the stone, and it would become a permanent part of him. I haven't studied the stones thoroughly, and I wouldn't have known how to use it, though I have to admit that now I'm getting curious. But let's return to your original question—why didn't the fog affect Daniel. The stone made Daniel. I don't know what exactly happened, but I can speculate that, thanks to that, Rex couldn't control Daniel. The stone didn't want to hurt Daniel. Daniel had a special connection with it. It was fighting Rex, and one way it could be successful was by not letting Rex control Daniel, the stone's own creation."

"What's with your eyes?" Ethan asked, watching the colour of Fortis's eyes. "They turned blue for a moment."

Fortis smiled and looked down. "As Rex's were, my eyes are also a little strange. It was one distinguishable trait of my kin. Years later, I learned to control it. I wanted to blend in. Sometimes my emotions momentarily overcome me, and the colour of my eyes changes, but I've got pretty good at controlling it. Anger doesn't control me anymore, neither does sadness. Other emotions are rarer, but also more difficult to control. Rex knew that he could control that glow in his eyes, but he didn't want to, because it distinguished him from 'the lesser races' as he called them," Fortis said, making air quotes with his hands. "I didn't want to be recognizable and memorable by a simple trait like that. Rex was always more egocentric. Having an ability no one else had made him feel superior."

Ethan remembered the glow in Rex's eyes. It was true that Ethan hadn't needed to know about Rex; just seeing his eyes was a dead giveaway of his evil intentions. On the other hand, Fortis didn't blend in, and his shiny armour wasn't the only reason.

"I have one last question," Ethan asked, remembering the army outside the city. "Why has your army come all the way here, yet I didn't get any notification of your intended arrival? We have a system for sending information to avoid situations like this."

"With a normal army, I'm sure your system works. We can travel faster than horses or birds. It would take humans weeks to travel the same distance we travelled. I didn't want to just appear in front of your gates. That would be rather rude, and since the fight was over, it wasn't necessary. I believe that you were informed that we just 'appeared' on the horizon," Fortis said, doing the quotes in the air again. "That's because we did— from human's point of view."

Ethan thought about this for a moment, trying to imagine the actual travelling. Then he gave up. He had more important things to do than to fathom magic and its uses. "What will happen next?" he asked.

"That's up to you," Fortis said. "Our army will return home, taking Morgour's body with us. I will discuss with the high order of The League the gem's future. You can continue with your life as before. I understand that you have had a very rough start to your reign, but you will be all right. All this fighting will help you find out what changes this country needs and which traditions are important to keep. John will be nearby to monitor and stop any further attacks."

"You make it sound so simple," Ethan said with a smile.

"It usually is," Fortis said, returning Ethan's smile. "Sometimes it only looks complicated. That's because sometimes we try to do everything alone. That's not always necessary."

Ethan looked towards the guards by the gate. John was slowly walking back to the castle, leaning against Christine. He was limping hard, but he looked happy. Lord Adrian was watching Ethan and Fortis, frowning slightly. Ethan couldn't express how happy he was to have Lord Adrian for a friend. He looked at the gates and spotted Lord Thomas, who was discussing something with Captain Stuart. Lord Thomas was scratching his chestnut beard and talking while Captain Stuart kept on nodding.

Lord Charles was standing nearby, deep in thought. He looked sorrowful. Mary was standing by him, leaning against his shoulder. She looked as if she had been crying a lot lately. Lucy was carrying a bowl of water from the well to the castle; she appeared to be in a hurry.

Ethan looked at the castle. Bess was watching the whole scene from the balcony on the second floor. When their stares met, he nodded to Ethan. It was weird to have a werewolf as a guest in the castle. Even weirder was the fact no one objected. This was probably the first time in the history of Norene that a werewolf was actually welcome there.

Ethan looked at Joan's window. He spotted her in the window next to the one in her usual room. She stood there, watching Ethan with a sad face. She blushed when he looked at her, but she didn't look away. His anger was gone; it had been replaced by sadness. He missed talking to Joan, though he wasn't sure if he could ever talk to her the same way he had before. He had to figure this out.

"Thank you for everything," he said as he turned to Fortis. "Please, take Rex's body with you. I will make sure that John is looked after well. He surely is welcome in Norene."

Fortis smiled, bowed slightly, and turned away. Ethan watched him leave, thinking about his next steps. Suddenly, he felt like his whole lifetime was in front of him. There wasn't anything he couldn't do.

"Everything's all right?" Lord Adrian asked, approaching him. Ethan nodded absentmindedly. "Are there any orders?"

"Yes," Ethan said, and he looked at Lord Adrian. "I have decided to create a committee of seven lords, a few of which we already have. Seven is such a nice number. And I have decided that women can inherit the duties and privileges of the rank of lord too. Send messengers to the families of Lord Eric, Jonathan, Robert, and John. John and Robert's wives can take up their duties until their sons are of age. Call Captain Stuart into my office. Plan that for three in the afternoon. I need to discuss with him new arrangements in the Royal Guards. There will now be only one army. I'm not giving a large portion of power to any one lord. Give me two hours, and then send Lord Charles to my office. I need to talk to him about Daniel's funeral. I want to have a special ceremony for Daniel and Lord James. They both deserve the highest honours."

"Where are you going now?" Lord Adrian asked, curiously, as Ethan stepped towards the castle.

"I need to have a word with Joan."

"Have you decided to ask her to stay?" Lord Adrian asked with a happy smile.

Ethan stopped and thought about this possibility. He turned the idea over in his mind and then realized that he rather liked the idea of Joan being there by his side, maybe some children running towards them. Yet he wasn't sure about her motives. And above all, he wasn't sure she would stay. He couldn't stand another refusal from her.

"I haven't decided yet," he said at last. "Ask me in two hours, and I'll tell you how it went," he added, and he stepped towards the castle.

THE END

Lightning Source UK Ltd.
Milton Keynes UK
UKHW011127291119
354427UK00003BA/111/P